The Offence of Grace

Jonny Halfhead

WARNING: THIS BOOK CONTAINS GRAPHIC DEPICTIONS OF
SEXUAL ABUSE YOU MAY FIND UPSETTING

ISBN: 9798672684123

DEDICATED TO A HERO – TJ EMERY

CONTENTS

THANKS TO

Helen, Daniel Moult, Jenny Williams, TJ Emery, Terri O'Sullivan, Michelle, Tammy, Sarah-Jane Page, John Viney, Lara Kaput, Setters Proofreading and Editing Services

PROLOGUE

When someone is open with you, looks you straight in the eyes and tells you that they were sexually abused by a family member, how do you respond to that?

When someone else tells you, through a mix of tears and outright anger, that a deeply trusted family friend sexually abused them, what words of wisdom can you offer them?

When a stranger has spent many years working through a personal hell and shares with you their experiences of being sexually molested by a trusted Elder in a congregation, how does your body language, facial expression and vocal phrasing have a continued effect on that person?

Surely, the way you react to what that person is telling you, says so much about you. Yet the reaction of most Jehovah's Witnesses is to openly deny the truth of what those brave and remarkable people speak. Most Jehovah's Witnesses would say nothing to their community – a community which blatantly covers over and mistreats victims of sexual abuse. Most would accuse these confessions as voices of apostasy.

Some do raise their voice. Many get disfellowshipped for it.

Silence from the listener is not enough anymore! Silence from the listener is implicit!

Those who speak from experience and those that listen and raise their voice are modern heroes and their voices must be heard. These are the voices I have heard, they are real, and they are the voices of heroes.

This is not a true story but fiction. It represents the trauma suffered by thousands around the world.

1 - I AM GRACE

I can feel the sand moving over my fingers as I try and softly draw my fingertips into the hot baking grains. A calming slight breeze dances over my skin, which responds by pimpling and raising up to meet the refreshing air. I can feel the hairs on my arms stand up to meet the wind and sway in its cooling and soothing engagement. I so much want to be at peace.

The sky is such a satisfyingly deep blue and the heat from the sun bathes my whole body in a comforting glow. There isn't a single cloud to interrupt the sky. I am at peace, relaxed and sinking into the beach towel beneath my body.

But my brain keeps getting in the way. I want to stay exactly where I am, but shocks of electric pain run through my torso straight up to my brain, like lightning against a dark grey sky. My thoughts and my imagination fight to keep control and keep me in this safe, relaxing and beautiful space. But again and again pain strikes through my body and my thoughts fight against me, switching between one small, quick, ugly moment and then back again into the sand and sun.

I can feel a trickle of blood secrete onto my leg and underneath my body. This is getting worse. The pain; the blood; the feel of internal skin tearing and cutting with searing pain. My mind fights with itself trying to move between two realities. For a moment I win back control and once again I can feel the grains of sand between my fingers and I can see the deepest blue in the sky which fills me with hope and relief. I want to scream out so very loud but that will smash the glass; break the scene; land me back into the room from where I'm trying so very hard to escape.

Moments move violently back and forth. I win over the pain and intense fear and land myself back in the comforting sun only to be stabbed in the stomach by a sharp pain again. I can feel a breath against my ear and the blood rushing more intensely around my thigh and into the fabric underneath me. Each time reality makes me understand my true predicament. I want to shout out! I want to thrash out! I want to fight! But I feel so weak and vulnerable: I fear for my life. In my heart I know that if I just go back to the beach, back to the soothing sand and the warming sunshine, I will survive. I will live. This will end. This will be over. I just need to escape again.

Thankfully, I return to the beach. I curse the weakness of my own mind and imagination. In the real world I'm on my stomach, my face pushed down and squashed flat into the duvet. In my escape, I'm lying on my back, my stomach basking in the warmth of the sun. I hate myself. I can't even imagine my own escape convincingly. I hate my weakness. I hate it that I cannot keep myself on this beach for more than a minute at a time.

I stare at the dark blue sky. Its rich intense colour is hypnotising. I fix on one spot of deep blue and try to lose myself in it. I ignore the violent thrust jolting my body, I ignore the mixed smell of filthy sweat and blood and push myself deeper into that one blue spot. I roll my hands into the sand beside me and feel its coarseness between my fingers. I must remain fixed on this beach.

I stabilise myself and fix my gaze on that one spot in the deepest blue of the sky. In my peripheral vision I see a quick flash of white light. I struggle and fight with myself to keep my concentration, to not be distracted even though I can sense the distant growing of whatever it is far away. The pain subsides a little and I manage to keep myself held back, locked away in this better world. My concentration and focus keeps me away from my brutal reality and yet it feels as if my thoughts are drifting in circles within myself.

I think of God. I remember to pray and feel the sudden need to confide in Jehovah and ask him for rescue and help. I feel the warmth and love of Jehovah and I start to say his name and plead for his help and forgiveness. There must have been something I did wrong that has brought me to this place, and I want Jehovah to forgive me for whatever it is that I have done. I pray out loud for his guidance and for his love: "Please God, please rescue me from this pain and humiliation."

In the deepening blue sky, I struggle to concentrate between my discussion with God and trying to ignore the growing spectre closing in from the distance. I can feel a cooler breeze brushing over my skin from the direction of the growing shadow. My escape is being ruined; my concentration drawn away. Maybe this is God coming to rescue me? The distraction becomes too great to ignore and I turn my head to look.

The whole sky to my left is full with a growing storm. It was a beautiful but also a sinister sight. The white clouds in the foreground broke against the deep blue of the sky above me, but inside the storm the clouds turn into a dark and frightening grey. I am confused: was this Jehovah coming to rescue me? Or was my mind just not able to keep me away from reality?

It is then that a huge lightning strike rips through the storm cloud and hits close by on the beach. At the same time a stabbing pain goes through my stomach and up to my head. It is obvious that I am not able to keep myself away from my reality: I am not going to survive. I feel the cold wind picking up and moving the sand across my body. The skin pimples of relief that I had once felt now turn to a chill of dread and absolute fear. I call out to Jehovah for help and strength. I feel the chill across my skin like the hand of death crossing over me. I become aware again of the blood running down, inside my thigh. I can smell the vapour of sweat and blood in the air. His sweat.

I'm going to die; I now know it. The storm grows larger and larger, taking over the sky. The sun has now gone and there is little left of the beautiful blue sky. I implode with fear and tears, my body gives up with a slump and a deep sigh. I cannot take anymore; this is the end. The cold wind envelopes me, picking up the sand and whipping my skin and scouring me.

Then, like an answer to my prayers, everything stops. My assailant promptly leaves, and I stay watching the storm grow with an ever-greater ferocity and darkness. I call out again to Jehovah to rescue me and free me from the death facing me. I feel so alone, so ashamed and I pray for an answer as to what I have done to have been punished so badly.

I lay crying. I am alone – cold, bruised, bleeding and hurting so badly.

Eventually I come back to the world I no longer wanted to live in. I notice the evidence around me of my shame and humiliation and I make sure I clean, scrub and dispose of every bit of it. I am so very alone.

2 - ISOLATION

It's been six months. I'm crying my eyes out yet again in my bedroom. I feel so isolated in this small room. It feels so dark and lonely here. I feel the fear running through me like an acid coursing through every limb. I know I'm in trouble again, I know my mother is about to come through that door and go crazy at me. I just wish everyone in the world would simply disappear and leave me be. Or it would be even better if I could find just a little courage and stop my suffering in my own way, take control and end the constant pain.

It's very cold outside under the orange glowing streetlamps. I know that there's a whole world out there, yet it feels even more cold and lonely than it does in this room with my own solitary company. There are times when I think about the billions of people outside my window that are just going about their lives. I know that amongst them must be some kind, caring and loving people. But the vast majority of them are not Jehovah's people, and because of that they are all facing extermination very soon. Befriending any of them would be futile.

I think about the pending apocalypse. I've actually been praying for it to come. I don't care whether I'm on the side of the saved or not: the bliss of oblivion would be a most welcome comfort. I know I'm a disappointment to my family, to my parents. I feel so dirty and so guilty all the time. The trouble I get in is just an inevitable consequence of already being sinful and wrong.

I can hear footsteps coming up the stairway of the house. This is it. My mother is going to come through my bedroom door any minute now, fuming and mad as hell with me. If I had gone through with my plans an hour ago, I wouldn't have to face any of the inevitable punishment. I'm so tired both physically and mentally, I've had enough. I want life to stop and leave me be. My body aches and my stomach still stabs with pain and bloody reminders. I had held a knife on my wrist and pressed down enough to leave a faint mark that reminded me how pathetically weak I was. Just a few minutes, that's all it would have taken, and I would have had peace. Instead I deserve everything I know I will have coming to me. God will punish me and it will be justified.

The footsteps continue down the hallway and stop outside my bedroom door. I can tell by the pattern of the footsteps that it is my mother. My dad walks so much heavier and with less care and thoughtfulness. My mother tends to hover and glide, which makes her footsteps lighter and softer. My mother and I use to get on so well, even just a few months ago. We were the best of friends. I miss those days. I miss my mum.

The bedroom door handle turns and slowly and considerately the door is opened. I cower down into the mattress, lifting the duvet cover up to my face. I hate myself so very much, I hate the world I live in and I even hate my parents. I can feel the tears welling up again in my eyes as the door opens wider. I am in so much trouble.

The light from the hallway shines into my dimly lit bedroom as the door slowly moves open. From behind the door my mother's face appears, solemn, sad and caring – strangely not the angry face I expected.

"Can I come in and talk to you my little cherub?" says the soft and caring voice that I just didn't expect. It's the voice of the mum I used to know and not the voice I've been hearing these past few months. I cannot answer. I fear that any word that comes from my lips would open a torrent of uncontrollable tears. I hold still, grasping the duvet up to my lips tighter and tighter.

My mother steps into the room gently. She walks lightly across the bedroom closing the door behind her and drifts almost silently across the room to my bed. She sits down next to me and looks me straight in the eyes. I struggle to look back at her, I feel so much shame and guilt. Because my mother is sitting on the duvet, it pulls against my grip of the other end of the sheet, so I battle silently to keep it up to my face and cover my guilt and shame. I want to shout out and scream, I want to hold my mum and let it all just blast out without care or control, but every fibre in my body must fight that instinct. Instead, I look down at a fixed point on the carpet next to the bed.

I can see from the corner of my eyes that my mother has fixed her gaze on me. She gently lifts her hand and brushes the hair away from my face. The sudden touch makes me jump a little, I just hadn't expected this at all.

"I hope you know how much I love you, my beautiful daughter," says my mother's soft, gentle and soothing voice. "I'm so sorry that it's taken me so long to actually realise what is happening with you." I try not to react in anyway. How can my mother possibly understand me?

"I found the knife in the bathroom."

Oh no! I left the knife there only a short while ago, what an idiot I am! My mind races wildly – why did I leave it there? And then I realise, there's likely a bit of blood left on it too. I try and twist my wrist away from my mother's view so that it hides under the duvet cover which is lifted up to my face.

The blood on the knife means nothing on its own.

"I know for the past few months you haven't been yourself. A lot's been happening lately and you've been acting up too. I know we've had a few arguments and disagreements, but you know you can talk to me about anything at all, no matter what it is that's troubling you."

There's a moment of silence. I can hear the wintry wind blowing the branches of the trees around in the street outside. The noise just emphasises the silence in my room. I want to tell my mum everything, but I deeply fear the consequences of saying anything at all. I am 15 years old, a recently baptised Jehovah's Witness that has made a promise to God and his family. What happened to me six months ago happened for a reason and the fault is very likely my own. I deserve any punishment I suffer. If I confess and tell my mother anything, I could so easily be disfellowshipped; cast out from the congregation. The shame for my family would be as bad, if not worse, than the shame I currently feel. My mother would have to shun me. My immediate world of friends and family, everyone I know, would have to turn their backs on me and put me through a deserved penitence.

The silence between the two of us is unbearable. I want so much to hold my mother. She used to be my best friend. Only a few months ago I could tell her anything at all. No problem seemed too great between us. But that has now passed.

My mother puts her arm around my shoulders and gently pulls me to her. I fight myself to not break down.
"I've been watching you and thinking about you a lot this past couple of weeks." Her voice breaks softly over the rattling sound of the wind against the window.

"I think I've failed you as a mother. I expected that there may come a time when we would lose the close bond we've had as you've grown up. But instead of working through it, I got annoyed with you when your behaviour started to change. I should have been asking why it changed, but instead I took it personally and I was wrong, so wrong. Please forgive me."

There is a small window of hope that just maybe she understood and that we could work it all out, but I immediately shrugged off that possibility. My mother was always an easy target to take out my frustration and anger on. I always regretted being like that, but I also felt betrayed that somehow, she didn't automatically know, that she hadn't sensed or empathically realised straight away that my life wasn't right. So, I unfairly attacked her for it.

I am so tempted to do the same thing again. I don't want to tell her anything and yet at the same time I wish I could confide in my best friend like I always used to. It feels just like those times when my mother would check up on me at night while I was in bed sleeping. Occasionally I would be awake and aware that she had quietly come in to check I was sleeping. I would lie there wanting to be fussed and told "goodnight", but I would not move a muscle and pretend to be asleep. I would even fake-snore. Why would I do that? Why am I ignoring her motherly affection now, why don't I just talk to her as she holds me? I feel so much internal conflict.

I can feel my mother shaking as she tries to carry on softly speaking to me:

"I... I've noticed a pattern...and I'm afraid to even think what it might mean."

I feel uneasy, I sense the conversation is getting too close to my carefully kept secrets. I pull away from my mother's arms, yet her grip is more than I expected. Instead of letting me go, she calmly tightens her grip and holds me warmly and firmly.

"When we go on the preaching work, you always hold back and start to delay and cause trouble. Then, when we meet up before going out on the work, there's a pattern I have noticed that depends on whether you play up more or just accept that we knock on doors and talk to people about God. I did think that you were rebelling against going out and meeting people on the door to door work. I know how daunting it can be, especially when it's the local area and we knock on doors where someone from your school could be on the other side of those doors."

Then, silence, as my mum gathers her thoughts. I can tell by the soft way she speaks that she's trying so very hard to use the right words and tread delicately. I am reluctant, though, to sit and hear where the conversation is leading to. I can feel the pain in my stomach growing. I struggle against my own mind throwing pictures and memories at me that I just don't want to see or think about, not even for a split second.

Her grip on me is tight as she breathes a large sigh and then carefully continues:

"For a few months I was determined that my little girl was rebelling, that perhaps the girls at school were influencing you to play up, or that you were getting bullied at school and you were afraid to face them when you are out with us on the preaching work.

"I'm so mad with myself that I was too lazy to look properly. But when I did take a step back, I started to watch you and notice that you were very upset when a certain person would be in the group that day."

A cold shiver goes through my spine. My mother knows, she has worked it out.

Then once again, silence. The window continues to rattle

from the strengthening wind outside. I feel chilled, guilty, isolated and frightened, as though I've been found out, that my evil sin has been discovered and I'm exposed to the whole world as a traitor and a filthy sinner. I feel as if I don't deserve to be in the warmth of the maternal grip I find myself embraced in.

I hear myself saying over and over in my head: "don't say his name, don't say his name" as though the very whisper would invoke a mighty demon to devour me whole. The whole room starts to spin as though I'm on a merry- go-round, adding to the nausea welling up from the pit of my stomach. Not a single fibre of my being wants to face the truth. I don't want to think about any of it.

The dim lights in the room seem to flicker and I cannot work out if it's me that's on the verge of passing out or the storm outside playing havoc with the electrics. I don't know whether to rip from my mother's arms and just run into the storm, or to trust her as I once did and slip further into her warm embrace.

There's a tension growing within me as I wonder if she will say that name. The quiet inside the room grows like a shadow creeping up the walls. I can feel it coming. I can feel the air building up inside my mother's lungs as she prepares, slowly, to speak again. The world goes into slow motion. My head spins, my fingers tingle, my body turns cold and sweats. I want to stay in this uncomfortable but predictable position where the monster from my nightmares isn't named. I know in my mind that there is no healing without confrontation, yet the whole of my body and heart just cannot comprehend the eternal darkness that may follow if that name is spoken.

I'm struggling between flight and pushing against my mother and shutting her up. The faint hope of a loving relationship with my mum, the relationship that once was, holds me in limbo. While I go back and forth in my head fighting with the two extremes inside of me, my mother makes the choice for me.

"Kris! It's Kris isn't it?"

There it is. The monster is named. Those four simple letters shatter the air along with my heart, my head and my body. I sink further down into my mother's firm grip, down into her flesh, into her bosom. There's a world of darkness pressing down on me as I feel the torn flesh in my lower stomach weep again with blood. My body reminds me it seems as though it wishes to torture me. The storm that was once outside has whipped through the confines of the windows and walls of my bedroom and now howls around our embrace.

I don't want to acknowledge anything, but I know that even in my silence I have given everything away. I feel exposed, cold, shamed and guilty. The grip my mother has on me never falters. It fills my very soul with a comfort to the point that my tears start to well up from deep in my chest. I don't want to cry. I don't want to give this situation even more substance than it already has. Although the moment to take flight has gone, I cannot help using all my strength just to hold on against my cascading emotions.

My tears are like a tap filling a bucket. They fill and fill and fill. You try to hold them but it's just pointless and the welling expansion is impossible to fight against. I can feel my blood pressure soaring up to my head. My spine feels cold, clammy and sweaty and yet my face feels hot, red and puffy. The surf is building and the inevitable is going to happen.

I choke and burst with an uncontrollable flood of tears in the comfort and warmth of my mother's embrace.

3 - DUAL

It's been four weeks. I've tried to be the girl I used to be, the girl that loved her mother and family and would do anything for them. I know inwardly that I expect everyone to just realise what was happening to me. I expect them to know the kind and warm-hearted girl I used to be and to know that if I was acting up, then there would be a damn good reason for it. I resent the fact that my family didn't know straight away when my character changed. I also resent the fact that it took my mother so long to work it all out. I'm angry with them all and that anger manifests itself.

I don't really understand myself, why I pretend to be bad, why I shout and talk back all the time, why I flirt and pretend to be dangerous and rebellious. This stronger and louder personality has become a comforting habit that I can't seem or want to break away from.

Although talking to my mum has brought me a little closer to her, I can't just, overnight, return my personality to what it was – and why would I? Nothing has changed at all. The daily and weekly routine is still the same. I still see and interact with the same people whether I want to or not. I still go to the Kingdom Hall twice a week. I still see Kris, smiling, hugging people and carrying on with not a care and still occasionally throwing glances at me across a crowded and busy room. Every time he throws that glance, I freeze. If he catches my eyes, I feel isolated, cold and alone. Every time it happens, I'm extremely angry with myself for looking at him and adrenaline pumps through me like an acid that makes me feel sick, dizzy and shaky. Why do I look at him to even allow that connection to happen?

It's so much more satisfying for my personality to be loud and angry. In some ways it keeps people away and it helps me have fun and try to forget who I am and what has been done to me. I cannot help but resent my mother as well. I suppose I have put her into a no-win situation. I don't want anything done about Kris except perhaps to keep him away from me. I don't want anyone else to know what has happened to me because it's no-one else's business. It's my shame, my pain and belongs to no-one else. But then at the same time, Kris is walking around still haunting me, still occasionally touching me and humiliating me in public. Every time I step into the Kingdom Hall I want to scream at the top of my voice and destroy all the bad in the room with a scream so loud and deadly that only the innocent could survive it.

I have thought every day about not going to the Kingdom Hall. Each time, twice a week, we get close to preparing to go and I consciously start acting up. I do not want to attend the meeting, but both my parents insist that I must. They keep telling me how my life and my future depends on going. To be honest the pain I feel every time I step into that building makes me want to sacrifice the long term to save the unbearable pain in the short term.

It was a couple of evenings ago, after coming back from the Kingdom Hall that my mother sat me down quietly in my bedroom and told me the news I had been dreading. My mum had reported my "allegations" to the Elders and they had arranged for an investigation to be carried out.

I can't believe my mum used that word.

Allegations!

She hadn't used that term before and it was obvious that a meeting with the Elders had moved my mother's absolute belief in me, to a state of all-round doubt and questioning. I could see in her eyes that the initial anger aimed at Kris had gone and instead the "Christian way" had taken over. I was as much of a suspect as Kris was now. If I knew exactly what was coming my way, I thought I needed an ally with as much anger as I had inside of me.

For the past two days I have been in an absolute hell dreading today. I had heard before of rumours within the congregation of judicial hearings around wrongdoing. I had older friends that laughed and joked about being dragged in front of the Elders and being interrogated. Those stories always sounded horrific and soul-destroying, even though their recall amongst friends was done against a backdrop of laughter and bravado. I didn't want to be questioned. I wanted to be left alone and not have to see Kris ever again. I wanted him to just go away. I don't know what I expected of my mum. Part of me deeply regretted saying anything to her, but I'm also intelligent enough to know that my new personality, my devilish acting up, is a subconscious cry for help that I struggle to control and stop from shouting out loudly.

We are waiting in the car, on a cold dark night in the car park of the Kingdom Hall. My mother takes off her gloves and grabs my hand and turns to look at me.

"I'm with you. I believe you. Shall we say a prayer before we go in and ask Jehovah for his help and guidance?" Everything in this life is wrapped up and controlled around prayer. I find it difficult to ask God for help knowing he was there when it all happened. If Jehovah is there listening to my prayer, why doesn't he just sort out this injustice and save a lot of time, heartache and effort? I don't even have to ask the question; I already know the answer. It's been drilled into me for several years. The story of Job. Job suffered because it was a test of faith. I have to go through this test to show the strength of my faith. It's so very difficult to hate the process, hate my parents, hate the Elders, hate Jehovah and hate Kris. What is so much easier is just to hate myself. All that other hate is tiring.

The rain is battering down on the car and making a lot of noise. It's so cold that I'm shivering. My mum squeezes my hand tighter. I can't help but wonder where my dad is in all of this. I wonder if my mum has said anything to him at all. He hasn't treated me any differently than normal, so I doubt it.

There's an outside light on the Kingdom Hall, flickering and distorting through the rainwater running down the car windscreen. There's only one other car in the car park. It belongs to one of the Elders. But I know we are not to go into the Kingdom Hall until at least one other Elder turns up, otherwise the gathering would be deemed "inappropriate". So, we sit here and wait: wait for the trial to begin. I have no idea how this will go. I don't have a clue what the rules are, how things are done. I'm so nervous that I feel sick to the core of my soul. I wonder if God does actually know the pain I'm going through. I wonder if he cares.

A car pulls off the main road, up the side street and into the car park followed immediately by another. The rear car's headlights scan across the Kingdom Hall, then the car park and then the car in front of it as it parks. As the headlight glides through the rain it looks like a search beam on a coastal lighthouse scraping across the stormy sea. The beam picks out the silhouette of the passengers in the first car. I can see there are two people in the first car, two black figures against the bouncing reflections beyond the car park. There were only supposed to be three Elders in the judicial process.

My mind is doing leaps and circles trying to work out something that's screaming at me. What is my fear warning me off? There are supposed to be five of us altogether. Myself and my mother and three Elders. One Elder is already in the Kingdom Hall and two cars have just pulled in and parked. But the first car clearly has two people in it. That means six people in total. What is going on?

A cry in the far reaches of my subconscious is trying to escape. My subconscious knows what this is, but my conscious mind fights it. I close my eyes; this is not happening!

I squeeze my eyes tightly closed and inadvertently grip my mum's hand even tighter as my body starts to slip down the car seat. I bury myself in the footwell of the car and want to stay there.

"Oh no," I hear my mum say as the car doors slam shut and footsteps scurry over to the Kingdom Hall.

My mother's exclamation says it all. I know what's coming. I keep my eyes closed shut. I can feel the tight grip on my mother's hand slip as she starts to pull her hand away. The rain seems to be intensifying on the car roof. I just want to die. I can't face who is in that building.

I know how women are treated in this religion. They are supporters, second division helpers. No woman has any position of authority. They are given no responsibilities in the congregation. They are there to provide and nurture families. All the time in our bible studies, women are responsible for the downfall of man, for the sin of the earth. All women do is lure good holy men into wrongdoing. They even lured angels down from heaven and corrupted them with their beauty and sexual power. I knew in that building, as a woman, I would be guilty first and foremost.

My mother pulls against my tight grip to retrieve her hand. I don't want to go in there. I don't want to face my future. The almost predictable comes out of my mother's mouth.

"It's a test. Let's face it head on and together. Jehovah will bless us and guide us through."

It doesn't help that either everything bad I expected to happen is happening as I feared or that things are getting even worse. I regret saying anything to my mother. I should have kept my mouth shut. I should have just disappeared. Can anywhere else in the world currently be worse than here and now? I resist my mother's pull. I don't want to move at all.

"In a couple of hours, this will all be behind us. Be brave for just a couple more hours" My mum says kindly and softly. Her words reach straight into my heart and pull me up out of my despair for just a second. It's enough for me to get out of the footwell and sit back up into the car seat.

"Take a deep breath." We both get out of the car and into the cold and the rain to make the mad dash across the car park to the main doors of the Kingdom Hall.

We go through the main doors and into the lit entrance way, but no-one is there. The whole building is quiet, cold and empty. I can hear a few far off whispers the other side of the main doors and I see a dim light through the gaps in the door frames. My mum leads me through the main entrance doors into the main hall. I visit this place twice a week and it's always full of my spiritual family. A hundred people I intimately know and mostly love. But now it's empty and only partly lit. The air feels damp and cold. It doesn't feel at all like a holy place. There's an air of subdued spirits that hide in the darkness at the far end of the hall. I feel as though I'm being watched and studied as I follow my mother slowly across the main room to the second and smaller meeting room across the way.

A minute ago, I didn't want to move. Now I feel like a thousand ghosts are watching me just out of view, as though their very hands are reaching out and touching my shoulder as I speed up my pace to reach the far room. Waiting at the entranceway to the meeting room is one of the Elders, dressed in his full suit as though it was a regular meeting night. I wonder if these people ever live outside of their ties, shirts and suits.

The brighter light from the smaller room lights up the way. The Elder extends his arm out to greet my mother and guide us into the meeting room. I look down, I will not catch his glance, I will not look into his eyes. I feel intense fear and unbelievable shame as though I have made up lies and an entire story just to hurt other people.

I'm hit with the smell of an electric fan heater that seems to be burning more dust than electricity. The burning odour becomes overwhelming.

I hold my head down with my eyes to the floor. I see there are four pairs of legs in that room instead of three. My mind races again trying to work out who the fourth person is. Surely my trial isn't to be heard by four Elders? That's not proper at all. Maybe this is serious enough to warrant four Elders instead of the usual three.

There is another more sinister thought running around my imagination. A dark and deep dread of a thought so awful that my heart and mind struggle to supress those thoughts away from my overactive subconsciousness. The Elders love me. This whole meeting is set up with love and care to look after my physical, emotional and spiritual future and wellbeing. I trust them and I trust Jehovah. They wouldn't do what it is that stabs at my heart in its deepest recesses of dread and fear, would they?

I hesitate before I walk through the door, fearing who is on the other side. My mum tugs at my hand as I begin a resistance against her. I feel frozen and cannot walk into the room. My mum feels me stop and turns around to face me to try and re-assure me.

We both walk through the door and into the small room together. I keep my head and my eyes down to the ground. I lock my stare at my feet and the industrial hard carpet that covers the whole of the Kingdom Hall, like an old-fashioned hairy chequer board that stretches infinitely through the building. This time I feel resistance from my mum's hand, a sudden stop and a loud gasp of breath.

"No, no this isn't right. He cannot be here, this is wrong!" my mother shouts in a wild mix of fear, anger and tearful desperation. Those words strike through me like an electric shock. It is my worse and darkest fear being realised. Those very thoughts I battled internally with just a few moments ago have morphed into a morbid reality. I don't need to look. I can now feel him there, sitting in the room. I don't want to look, I don't need to look. Why then does my whole body fight with me to raise my head and see?

There sitting in the corner of the room is Kris. Fucking Kris! Dressed up like the Elders in shirt, tie and suit as though he just had to fit in with the rest of the club. The swearing, screaming and hatred running through my head along with the sickening adrenaline, intense shaking fear and deepest pit of dread, fuels my anger and nausea. I don't look long enough to catch his eyes. The sudden heat of anger burns itself out. My glazed acceptance instead sinks back down to the floor. I have now died. My insides have died. My life is over, and I am now witnessing my own living hell of which there is only one escape.

My mother pulls at my arm. There's a small and quick scurry as my mum tries to turn around and pull me back out the room towards the door, but the way is blocked by one of the Elders.

"Kris has every right to meet his accuser and hear the accusations against him face to face. This is Jehovah's guided way. Please sit down," says one of the Elders calmly but firmly as he shuts the door behind us stopping my mother and I from escaping the room.

I can barely stand, and I collapse into my mother's embrace. She pulls me towards the two waiting chairs that are placed next to each other across from the four chairs opposing. Nothing here feels loving and fair. The atmosphere has suddenly turned hostile and accusatory. I can see the legs of the four chairs all next to each other in a row across from my mother and me. That alone gives me the worst fear of where the line of fairness has been drawn. Already it seems more than obvious that these four men have already agreed their verdict before I've even had the chance to open my mouth.

My mother and I sit down. The conference chairs are plastic and functional and are always uncomfortable. The act of sitting in one of those chairs forces you away from the person next to you and makes you sit upright and squarely facing forward. My mother still has a hold of my hand, but because of these damned chairs I now feel so very far away from her, more than ever. I try to lean across and get nearer to her, but the stubborn chair fights against me. Every time I shuffle in the chair, try and feel closer to my mother and less isolated, the pain from the awkward posture that is required in it, forces me straight, front and upright and alone once more. After a few shuffles I give up trying.

I sit, fighting inside my head. I want the world to swallow me up, or even better I could melt into the floor and just die right here. I'm trapped, unable and powerless to do anything except face what has been thrown in front of me. One half of me wants to stand up and shout out so loud that everyone's head in the room explodes. The other half wants to fight, throw my fists around in a mad frenzy and then run and never ever stop running.

The two halves of me fight for supremacy. The fast mood swings and the uncomfortable chair make me fidget and squirm. My eyes stay focussed on the floor, down and ashamed. In a fit of fury my glance flicks up straight into Kris's eyes giving him a dirty, devilish and even flirty look. I'm just starting to get the confidence to take a hold of the situation in my head, to be aggressive and control the situation my way, when sense and reality and my mother's grip on my hand swing me violently back to feeling cold, alone, ashamed and isolated. I can see the look on the Elder's face as this internal battle rages in me, making me look as though a demon is thrashing at my insides. I can see in their eyes their judgement and their disgust before anything has been said. They have already made their verdict. They have already decided the course of proceedings. My mother and I are women and as such have no power, no say and no influence over anything that is about to happen.

One of the Elders starts to speak and has clearly taken the lead in the room. He suggests that we all bow our heads in prayer to ask for Jehovah's guidance over the coming judiciary. I see everyone bow their heads and all I can feel are the tears welling up in my eyes. I don't want to cry in front of them. I refuse to cry in front of them. I hate them all! I look at them while they have their eyes closed and heads down as the lead Elder says a prayer out loud asking Jehovah for guidance and all the usual language I hear at the Kingdom Hall every week. There is nothing personal, nothing loving, nothing specific about the pain and agony that's in the room in his prayer, just a list of prayer language phrases and tick boxes that always seem to go into most Kingdom Hall prayers. I don't feel any comfort from the prayer. I don't feel any guiding spirit descend. I don't feel a warmth entering the room, just the burning smell of fusty dust particles from the fan heater and the man-made fibres of the industrial carpet underneath the heater getting melting.

Why don't I feel anything? Is God here? Have I closed myself off from him? Has Jehovah abandoned me as well as the Elders? Have I now become the wrongdoer somehow?

As everyone has their eyes closed, heads bowed and praying, I cannot help but feel angry and resentful of everyone in the room, including my mum, who is the one that brought me here. I confessed to my mother in confidence and somehow she managed to twist me around to doing this. I did not want to do this at all.

When the prayer is over, the lead Elder starts to talk about what we are here for. He says that I have accused one of God's servants of doing the most horrific things and that the Elders must take the accusation seriously and properly investigate the matter. The lead Elder then insists on reading a few passages from the Bible, quoting them as guidance on how to run the judicial investigation. Each time he mentions a Bible verse, just like in a normal Kingdom Hall meeting, he asks everyone to open their own copy and read the passages with him. One of his fellow Elders reads a passage. One passage he asks my mum to read and then he asks me to read the final one. I haven't brought a Bible with me. My mum brought hers along and she holds it between the two of us to share. I don't want to read anything. I can barely see through the masses of tears coating my eyes and because I'm trying so hard to fight those tears as well as the crushing adrenaline that is making me shake and feel very sick, I don't know how I can possibly read anything.

The text from the Bible is so small and my mum's hand is also shaking to the point that I just cannot see the passage clearly enough to read it. I manage to splutter out a couple of words, then my mum takes over, much to the annoyance of the lead Elder who partially grumbles under his breath. Once my mum finishes reading, he lets out an obviously unashamed sigh.

I understand the proceedings, I really do. The Elders, as God's representatives, must show they are doing things "by the book" and so must be seen to be using the Bible to back up and guide how things are done. It makes the proceedings so very cold and clinical. There seems to be an absence of warmth and care here. I feel like I have stepped into the middle of a political quarrel and not a moral one at all. My mind and imagination run away at a tangent, so very eager to get away from where I am and the foreboding subject matter that I'm sure I will be asked about very soon. Before I know it, I'm busy forgetting where I am and trying to work out, in the logical part of my brain, how Elders deal with the conflict of morals and politics. They must face it all the time. If there are three people here, how do they ever agree on anything? Even though I belong to such a strict and closed society with very defined rules, I still struggle to find two people who agree on the real nitty gritty of grey areas and personal opinions.

I'm so relieved to be thinking at a tangent inside my own head, to be somewhere else except in this room. Then I'm suddenly jolted back into reality again by my mum pulling at my hand. I look up at the faces in the room all looking at me as though they are waiting for a word.

"Sorry," I say sheepishly, "could you repeat that?"
I know I'm not doing myself any favours, but then I don't see the point of any of this anymore. Because of Kris's presence, there is an air that a decision has already been made, that I'm the one on trial and that this is just a matter of formality.

One of the supporting Elders actually speaks.

"Please tell us and Kris, what it is that you are accusing him of. We want to hear from you directly."

"This is ridiculous!" my mum loudly jumps in, "this is bordering on abuse in itself!"

The lead Elder leans forward on his chair towards the two

of us and says slowly and deliberately, "We are appointed by Jehovah. Are you accusing three of Jehovah's appointed Elders, appointed by his spirit and by the Governing Body to do his work and to look after his flock, of abuse as well?"

My mum backs off and sits back into her chair. I can clearly see how hard those words hit her. You do not question the Elders. I'm surprised my mum had the guts to have a go at them like that. I squeeze her hand this time as a sign of support from me and as an apology for letting my mind drift away.

The room goes silent and still. The only sound in the room is the whirring of the fan on the tiny heater working overtime to try and pierce the fierce cold in the room. I feel like that heater. Alone and working overtime in a pointless endeavour. I'm not going to win here at all. It's all my fault and I am to blame. The Elders are clearly showing me my mistake and therefore Jehovah is guiding me to see how wrong, dirty and evil I am.

I hate the silence in the room. Everyone is waiting for me. I have been given my turn to speak and yet I'm still fighting a civil war inside myself to either forget it all and just run out the room or to face up to my abuser. I just don't know if I have the strength for either option. I'm still waiting for the ground to swallow me up. Yet, for as long as I wait, there seems to be no sign of that happening.

I cannot stand the silence drilling into my temples like a jack hammer. I try and speak but my head and heart are fighting so fiercely that I just don't know who I am anymore and have no idea what to say. I pull my gaze up from the floor. I can't just study the pile in the stuffy carpet through tear-filled eyes.

I look up and see across from me,

Kris.

He is sitting almost slouched down his chair as though he owns everything that is happening in this room. Just the sight of him starts to make me angry and I can feel a sharp stab of pain in my lower stomach as a reminder. I feel sick from the fear and adrenaline, but the added pain from my insides gives me a focus and a relief from the anxiety. I suddenly feel angry. I suddenly feel pissed off at the smug bastard that's ripping my life apart sitting right there in front of me. The look on his shitty little face as though he controls and owns me. Fuck you Kris!

"You....you abused me, hurt me, used me and I hate you, I hate you!"

I didn't shout. I controlled and looked him straight in the eyes as I said it. It took all my strength though and I retired back again into my chair as three gasps leapt from the Elders and I hear my mum start to cry. I return my gaze to the floor. There! I did it, now leave me alone and do what you must.

Everyone shuffles around uncomfortably on their chairs. The silence has been broken and ripped up. I start to disappear back into my own imagination once again and try to stop the internal fighting inside. I have made my statement, now I can only move forward. I have a sense of pride and yet a deepening fear of retribution. I have stepped forward. It was very likely that there was only lots more pain to come. At least though none of it would be from Kris.

The lead Elder breaks the silent air once again:
"You know Kris is a Ministerial Servant, a man with earned respect in the congregation and in the eyes of Jehovah. You know he is a happily married man with a beautiful wife. You went to his wedding with everyone else in the congregation. Weren't you a bridesmaid? Why would you say something like this? It breaks my heart to hear you accuse Kris of something so serious."

As I suspected, those words were hardly impartial.

"We need to ascertain what exactly you are accusing Kris of. We need to know the details of everything you believe has happened. Because of the nature of what you are accusing, we will have to go into great detail, I'm afraid, to ascertain what guilt, if any, there is to face up to. So please start from the beginning and tell us everything. Remember that Jehovah is listening and he will know if you are lying. You know the punishment is great from Jehovah if he sees that you are lying or trying to deceive the very people he has put here now for you to speak only truth to."

I don't understand what is being asked of me to even start to speak. What is meant by the word "detail"? How far do they want me to go? Once again I want to just clam up, roll up into a ball and ignore the world completely. I don't want to be a part of this. But so much time this evening has already passed, and I know what this is. The Elders won't give up, they won't just let me forget it. They wouldn't even let me retract anything either. I'm in too far already to take it back. I may as well just move forward and get this hell over with. Jehovah doesn't seem to be with me today and after swearing like that inside my head, I'm not totally surprised. Maybe they are right. Maybe I am demonised, maybe I have gone too far and need redemption.

"It..." I start slowly. "It started about a year ago. We were on the ministry and he touched me..." I squirm saying it out loud, hearing my own voice as though it was another person speaking. The room falls silent. "...and that's where it started."

Silence again. I drop my head and my eyes stare at the floor. My mum gently squeezes my hand in support and yet I still feel so alone, so guilty, so cold, isolated and exposed.

More silence.

"Ok, you have to give us more detail. You were on the ministry. With Kris?"

"Yes, I was put with Kris and we started to work through the houses, from one door where Kris would do the talking, then on the next house I would do the talking." The memories flash up in my head as I try and figure out which housing estate we'd been on and which day of the week it was. "I remember it was a warm day as I was wearing a dress with an open back just to my shoulder blade. At one house, when it was my turn to speak, as I knocked on the door waiting for someone to answer, Kris stroked the skin on my back."

Oh, that horrible cold shiver that followed Kris's fingers down my back jars my memories all the way down to the pit of my stomach. For a moment I dry heave and feel as though I am going to vomit. The memory of the heat of the sun that day almost turns it into a cold, black and white picture and I jolt myself from the shudder down my back, returning me to the small, dank room at the Kingdom Hall. I put my head in my hands. That was where it started. I recall the shock of confusion in my mind. At first, I'd thought it was a bug crawling on me and I swung around and Kris had the creepiest smile on his face. That look on his face – I recall it so clearly. Yet another shiver runs up and down my whole body and again I feel like I might vomit.

The lead Elder leans forward with eagerness, "What were you wearing that day? You said you had a dress on with a low cut back."

Did I hear that correctly? I'm so confused. I'm barely holding myself together recalling that first encounter. It was the day when everything changed, the day when I just didn't understand people anymore. I look over to my mother wondering if I'd heard correctly. My mind is running in circles and I'm struggling to keep any focus at all. I probably didn't pick that up right.

"Tell me what you were wearing, it was warm wasn't it?"

"I..." I look questioningly at my mum. I don't really understand the relevance of the question. Strangely though I do remember what I was wearing.

"I was wearing a summer dress. It was a quite a warm day. It was a white cotton dress with flowers on it."

"Would you say the back of the dress was low cut? Could you see your bra strap above the cut of the dress?" said the lead Elder in an almost accusatory tone.

"I don't understand. Why is that relevant? Mum, you know which dress I mean...?"

"It's only about four inches down from the neckline on that dress," my mum says turning to the Elders in an equally accusatory tone, "so, no, it doesn't go anywhere near the strap of her bra. How is this relevant?"

For the first time since the opening prayer and reading a Bible passage earlier, the third Elder actually speaks: "We need to get a full and complete picture to make sure we don't draw any unnecessary conclusions. Please go on."

I look over to my mum. This is all so confusing. What are they actually saying here? I try and look for an answer in my mother's eyes, but she just nods to encourage me to carry on. I turn back to the Elders and pick up again.

"That was the first time he did that. But a week later back on the ministry, I was put with Kris again, and he did the same thing: touched the skin on my back, only this time he also touched my hair." I don't want to carry on. My mind rushes so fast it's already moved ahead to some terribly dark and horrible places. I'm clamming back up. My gaze moves to the floor below me. I continue: "The first time could have been an accident, but this second time was purposeful. All I could think about was Julie. Kris has such a beautiful wife whom I love dearly and is a good friend, why would he touch me like that?"

The lead Elder sits back in his chair almost smugly. "Why did you think like that? He only touched you, tidied your hair. Why did you think of Julie? Was it perhaps that you were aroused by being touched by a good looking young married man and you felt guilty feeling that way?"

I can't believe the tone the lead Elder uses. He is accusing me of being aroused by what Kris was doing to me. I know what I felt. I felt sick when he touched me. It was so lechery and creepy. I was so shocked that Kris could be like that and because my brain runs like a runaway train, I immediately thought of Julie and how Kris was betraying her, my friend. At the time I was too shocked to be angry.

I'm stuck living in two places at the same time. The memory of Kris touching my skin and making my whole body crawl, like a spider scurrying over my bare skin, is nauseating. At the same time, I am here in this dank, cold room, scared and feeling so very oppressed. I'm not sure that I can clearly articulate how I feel now and, even less so, how I felt then. I can see the direction this whole conversation is going and I'm not sure if I care to even try and fight it. What power do I have against three Elders and against God himself if he is the one directing this interrogation? How can I possibly fight against God? I'm just a girl holding onto her mother's hand like it's a solitary lifeline.

Once again, the internal civil war rages within me. If I am cornered and guilty, then what do I have to lose to fight back with everything I have? I've had a lifetime of people telling me where my place is. I am female. I do not hold position, nor responsibility in the church, nor any power and I never will have. I am a servant of men. That is my place. That is where I am taught to be. The position I am told to keep and have respect for. To go against that regime is to go against God himself. As the world outside shouts out against inequality, I am told to be no part of that outside world and to get in line. Part of my recent rebellion has been against that very suppression and it gets me in so much trouble, to the point that it's all catching up on me now.

I just cannot win.

I look back up at the Elders and try and explain why I found Kris's fingers on my skin and hair repulsive and why it felt like he was the one betraying Julie not I. The rebellious tone in which I deliver it, though, does not sit well with my immediate audience.

"So, is that all that Kris did? Is there more?" says the lead Elder trying to counter and subdue my energy.

I know where the next part of the story takes me. I don't want to go there. I had put all my consciousness in another place so as not to be where we are heading right now. I'm trying desperately to concentrate my memory away from that day. Every so often, through the silence of the room, I get a flash that hits me in the middle of my forehead. It stabs me with an intense pain and flickering images that I just don't want to see. I feel like I'm in a boxing ring and being punched repeatedly in the face. I do not want to go there! I do not want to think about it.

I feel sick. My stomach turns over. I can feel my mouth watering like a tap has just turned on in the insides of my cheeks. I'm going to vomit. I feel dizzy and my head faces back down to the floor. The silence in the room is deafening. It screams in my ears so loudly that I want to scream back at it. I can feel my head move towards the floor below me and I start to slip from the chair I'm sitting on. I have no energy left. There's nothing left in me to fight with. I feel as though my soul is slipping away from me and leaving me to die. I feel like my last breath could just slip out from under me as my knees slide towards the floor in front of me.

Goodbye.

My mum feels my body slipping as I slump down in the chair and roll forward to the floor, knees first. She manages to grab my arm as I slip down to the ground and nearly gets pulled onto the floor with me. Only one of the Elders moves forward and tries to catch me and I'm caught in free fall by my mum and the Elder.

"Can we have a break please?" my mum pleads. With an exasperated exhale of breath the lead Elder reluctantly agrees.

I don't hear the mumblings and words said as I try to stabilise myself. The Elder that caught me, lifts me back up onto the chair, helping with my mother. Then he offers to fetch me a drink of water. I see the shuffling feet of the other two Elders and Kris walk past me and out the door. It's only a moment until my mother and I are alone in the small stale-smelling side room.

My mum fusses over me, asking if I'm ok. It takes a few minutes for me to stabilise and mentally come back into the room. I tell my mum I need to go to the toilet because I feel really sick and I run out the room and stagger quickly into the ladies' toilets.

As soon as I make my way into the cubicle, I stagger and drop to the floor nearly banging my head on the toilet seat. The cubicle is cold and very comforting as sweat starts to poor down my face. My whole body feels like it's trying to flush itself through my face. My throat spasms and pulls as I try and fight my body to stop it retching, but I lose the fight very quickly and throw up into the toilet bowl. As I retch with my head pulling and gagging from my body, I just can't stop images of Kris flashing and searing into my brain. This is a trauma I've tried so very hard to push away but insists on coming back in a strobe of flickers and snapshots of horror.

Once I stop retching, I turn and squeeze myself between the toilet and the wall. The wall and floor are so very cold but provide such sweet respite from the heat and sweat emanating from my head. I hit a spot of tranquillity. For a moment there is silence. The images in my head relent for a short while. My body stops shaking and spasming and I have calm.

I lay with my head back looking up at the ceiling. There is a peace that I just don't want to disturb. I can feel my stomach moving and churning under the strain it has just been ripped through. The sweat on my face starts to slow just a little so that the beads just sit on my face instead of rolling down it. I don't want to move at all. I know that any movement in any direction will trigger a change that will likely start everything up again, so I sit motionless. At least my mind is quiet as I purposefully study the lines and cracks in the ceiling. I can hear my mind starting to slowly wake up as I fight and insist that the concentration on the ceiling, its many lines and barely discernible patterns of painted brush strokes, keeps the madness at bay.

All my mental powers home in on the ceiling's painted texture: the lines, the sweeps, the swoops of evidence of numerous painted coverings. This is a communal building, looked after by the sweat and hard work of its volunteers and that evidence is on this ceiling. Layers and layers of the same white paint applied over and over by amateur volunteer after amateur volunteer. I will probably end up painting this ceiling white at some point.

My body begins to relax but I know the simplest twitch in my mind or body will have me straight back into sweating again like a torrent and feeling nauseous. I keep my concentration on the ceiling until it's broken by my mum's voice on the other side of the toilet door.

"Are you ok? Can you open the door please and let me see you?" accompanied by a gentle and quiet tap on the toilet door. As quiet as she knocks, I'm still jolted away from deep concentration. A jolt that rips through my stomach and immediately brings the sickness back. My face once again starts to drip with sweat and I become aware of the cold wall and the hard, cold floor. I fight to try and keep the peace I had just moments before, but I can feel that the more I fight the worse I'm getting. I love my mum, but I just want her to go away. I just want everyone to leave me alone.

As the sweat increases and the pains in my stomach start to churn again, I lose my mental hold. Instead of looking at the ceiling, I'm looking at the door and I can see in my mind my mum on the other side. My concentration has slipped, and I'm once again fully immersed in the here and now, the Elders, the stuffy room, Kris and revisiting my worse horror.

In frustration I kick the inside of the toilet door which bangs loudly in the tiled room. I can hear my mum jump in reaction and let out a small squeal. I leave a boot print on the inside of the door, so clearly defined and evident. My isolation collapses in around me, swallowing me up. The whole cubicle which had become bright and pure white closes in and becomes very dark. The echo of my outburst seems to linger around the building as though my frustration is being echoed back to me to make me feel small and pathetic. I suddenly feel like a child having a tantrum because it cannot have its own way. I become reflective. I'm certainly not spoilt and yet every part of my being wants to curl up into a ball and hide somewhere safe, warm and comfortable. I don't want to face the monsters.

My every fibre, my every bone, my every thought and every sense, rebels and does not want to go back in that room and be molested all over again!

Yes, I said it to myself. I am the one that has been wronged, I am the one being victimised all over again. I am justified to feel angry. Fuck the world!

I did it again. I swore in my head. I shocked myself. God will hear me. He will see me and know my thoughts. I'm not so innocent, am I? As if I didn't feel sick already, the inner turmoil starts up yet again. I have had wrong done to me. I know I have. I should not feel like this. And yet, I act like this, I lash out, I swear. I'm angry and I know I've become flirtatious and I don't really know why.

"Please open the door," a soft voice says again from behind the boot print on the door.

My mother's soft voice breaks the circle of perpetual thoughts. I feel so alone and isolated, but I know mum is there just a couple of feet away. Yet why do I fight against her? Just like a spoilt child I start to think in terms of blame and the fact that she brought me here and that where I am is partially her fault. I know deep down that is not true. It would seem that we are both powerless in a world of men. Like a boat thrown around by the whim and desire of others. It would be so easy to hate absolutely everyone in the universe, including my mother, including God.

I open the latch on the toilet door and my mum slowly presses the door back to reveal my slumped corpse squeezed between the toilet bowl and the tiled wall. She recoils as she smells the stench of vomit.

"This is ridiculous. Come on I'm taking you home." She reaches out to try and pull me out of the wedge I have found myself in.

My mother's words are such a relief. I don't have to go back into that room and face the Elders. I can go home and get in my bed. Yet I find myself stuck and so lethargic. I can hear voices in the background as the Elders have obviously stirred.

"Tidy yourself up. I'll be just a moment. You're not going back in that room tonight." My mother straightens herself up, wipes her face with the palms of her hands and straightens her hair, nods to me, then turns and marches out of the room.

I try again to get up off the floor. A warm home feels so inviting that it gives me just that little bit of hope, enough to rouse myself to my feet. I start to hear raised voices, first my mother's and then a loud but controlled retort. I don't want to hear, I don't want to know what they are saying. I just hope my mother can get us away from here. Part of me is tempted to try to strain and work out what words are being said and the tone of the argument, but I realise that I really don't want to know. I just want to go home. I purposefully flush the toilet so that I don't have the choice anymore.

I step over to the sink and wash my face. My eyes sting as the sweat and water mix and splash into my eyeballs. Although I don't look, I can feel my face staring back at me in the mirror, but I have no wish to converse with it. I turn my back on myself and start to pull and straighten my clothing. I'm probably going to see him for one last time as we try to get out of the Kingdom Hall. I will try my best to show that he does not have a hold of me, as futile as that seems. I'm going to hold my head up and taunt him with my defiance. I hate him.

I can hear my mother's distinct footsteps coming back quickly towards the ladies' toilet block. The door swings open. "Come on we're going," she says firmly and grabs my hand and leads me out so fast that I nearly trip over and fall. We have just two doors to navigate and then we can get in the car and go home. As we leave the toilet block and go back into the main hall, my mum, bless her, tries to stand between me and the gaze of the Elders and Kris. She gently puts her hand down to my lower back and pushes me in front of her and towards the exit door.

Initially I keep my gaze to the floor, head lowered in shame. Part way across the hall, my anger starts to swell up and I start to boil at being forced to cower in shame. As I quickly walk out, I lose my self-control for a moment and turn to where the Elders are standing, and I see Kris. I look straight at him and give him the most sarcastic smile I can muster, then head straight for the door and walk through and out into blissful freedom. As I go out into the cold, rainy and dark evening I hear one last loud and controlled boom of a voice say, "we will see you again on Wednesday."

Before I allow those words to register, I start to run into the rain, through the darkness and towards the car. I just want to get in the car and shut them all out. When I get there, I find the door locked and I pull at the handle desperate to get inside. My mum sees my panic and quickly walks to the car and opens it. I jump inside, slam the door and curl up on the passenger seat. It's only then when those words sink into my brain. This isn't over. I may have got away today but we will have to go back again in a couple of days' time. I look at my mum, wet through from the rain and she looks at me with such sad and sorry eyes, shakes her head   and   apologises.

4 - BASE

I'm sitting on this same plastic chair again. So much for getting away. The two plastic chairs my mother and I sit on haven't even moved in the last two days. The room is still cold and dark, the smell from burning dust on the electric fan heater mixes with the smell of our damp clothes as we have come in again from the pouring rain.

The rain.

It hasn't stopped for three days. It knows and reflects the nature of my heart. I cannot get any lower than this. Here and now must be my lowest point. I can barely keep my head upright. I have had two days to dread this evening, two days to fear and shake my very soul to the ground. I am being forced to relive experiences I didn't even want to be in the vicinity of when they happened. Now I'm even less inclined to be associated with those experiences again.

My mother explained to me why I had to be here. It made some sense yesterday. This moment here and now is the worst place, the lowest point. In a few hours it will be done and finished, and my mother will be at my side the whole way through it at least. I may be mostly alone and isolated, but I have some proximity to love at least.

The room is not as full. There is a chair that's empty across from the two of us. The other four chairs are not stamped into the floor on the same spot as two days ago like the two chairs we now sit in. It is obvious those four chairs across from us have been in use. The three Elders still sit in line roughly in similar positions, but that one chair lays empty, aligned in a row with the Elders' chairs. The absence of a body on that remaining chair seems ghostly. I can see no-one sitting across from me, and yet I can feel the presence of someone still there facing and looking at me, forcing my head to bow in shame towards the floor. With every fibre in my being I hate the power I seem to give over to Kris. The seat of the chair that he sat on looks as though it's bowing under the weight of a body that's not there. It's truly frightening and hardly a relief at all that the absence of his physical presence has made the situation any lighter.

I start to feel very nauseous once again. My heart sinks heavily to the floor. My gaze falls to my feet and the sweat starts to once again pour from my face. As with the time before, the Elders insist on starting by going through a prayer and again read a scripture or two. On this occasion my mum reads both of the Bible passages assigned to us to read, which leaves me with a little bit of time to try and find any strength I have left to at least be able to speak.

Once the formalities are finished with, the lead Elder takes over the session as before.

"As agreed, we have asked Kris to stay at home for this session in line with your wishes, which I think is very good of Kris to do. He has every right to be here and face his accusers and hear first-hand the accusations against him. Yet, because he is a kind and considerate brother, and he says he doesn't want to be the cause of any more unnecessary pain that you are putting yourself through already, he has very kindly agreed to stay away. Which I think Kris has to be respected and commended for." My mother lets out a small and controlled huff, which made the lead Elder stop for a moment and look at my mum with disgust.

"We did though, take the opportunity yesterday evening to talk to Kris ourselves in this room and he was very open and honest with us, which we are all grateful for. Kris is, and has been, a good and respected Ministerial Servant in the congregation for a few years now and will make a fine Elder one day soon. He loves his wife and he loves his congregation and has proved that love many times over. Jehovah has blessed him. He admitted to the instance you mentioned of, which was stroking your hair, and he said it was a one-time moment of weakness and that was all it was. We think he was very genuine in his remorse and regret. Kris also told us that nothing else has happened between the two of you since that unfortunate incident."

"So we just need you to go through anything else that you believe Kris has done to you and in as much detail as you can."

I cannot believe the barefaced lies and arrogance from Kris, an arrogance that fills me with extra energy to raise my head from looking at the floor below me. I can feel my mum gently squeeze my hand in encouragement. The nausea still makes me sweat. I take in the ambience of the room. The stink of the stale carpet, the odour of old paper and books that mixes with the burnt dust from the heater. The only sound in the room is the rain hitting the emergency door from outside, the rush of the wind and the constant and rhythmical whirring of the fan blades in the heater, straining as though it had been running for a hundred years and was ready at a moment's notice to clang to a halt.

My mind and heart wanted to run away just moments before. I wanted the earth to swallow me up. But I can feel a moment of that time passing. My angry self, my violent and oppressed alter ego begins to stir within me. I know, if my mind starts to engage and my memory begins to go through the photographic motion of recall, that my anxiety will increase exponentially. My anger gives me a spike of energy, a call for justice, a madness against the words of Kris and a seed of revenge against the oppression of the three men sitting before me.

This is NOT a trial of justice. This is not a trial of love. This is political manipulation and a den of lies and corruption. I don't feel God's spirit anywhere here. All I feel is the cold air and the dampness of my rain-soaked clothes.

As my internal battle rages inside my head and heart, the room is left in an uncomfortable silence. One of the other Elders speaks and breaks it:

"You must tell us more. You have made a very serious accusation against a Ministerial Servant and if you don't follow that up, we can only assume that you are doing this to harm him and give him a bad name. If that is the case then we will have no choice but to discipline you, even disfellowship you and you don't want that, do you? You are a baptised member of Jehovah's organisation and as such are subject to Jehovah's rules and principals. You know what happens to the disfellowshipped don't you? Your mother won't be able to speak to you, your family will have to turn their back on you. Your friends will not be allowed to associate with you. You will be banished from the congregation until a time of repentance, which could take months or even years. Think of the strain that would put on your mother, to live in the same house, to cook your food, but not be able to talk to her own daughter because of her selfish actions. You don't want to put your wonderful mother through that, do you?"

That statement was all I need. I am so fortunate to have such a loving mother. She would never treat me that way. We both know what the rules are, but I know that actions like that are not loving or caring. They may not even be God's way. Something here is so very wrong. Who really would be like that? I thought about it for a moment and I do know a few in the congregation that would be like that even with their own children.

The confusion starts to add to my anger. I can feel an energy picking me up inside and working against my lethargy. Saying nothing and wanting to hide away is not going to solve anything. In fact, it seems to be making things worse. The more I shrink back, the more power over myself I seem to lose and the more I give to these three men and, of course, to Kris.

That thought rings around inside my head. I had sunk so low, I had no self-esteem, no power over my own body or my own destiny. It feels as though people are waiting in line to strip me of dignity, to strip me of life. Bless my mother; she has helped me through this, she has listened and reacted. Although I'm in turmoil because my mum has convinced me to be here and face these monsters, I know deep down that she believes that facing fear and facing persecution is the only right thing to do. I just didn't have the strength to do it on my own. And now the Elders are backing me into a corner. They are actually accusing me of making this all up and are threatening me, threatening my mother and threatening my family because of what Kris has done.

The adrenaline rushing through my body starts changing its effect on me. Just a few moments ago it made me feel sick and nauseous. Now I can feel anger starting to pick up that adrenaline and feed on it. There's another fight brewing inside my body: just minutes ago, I wanted to be sick from fear, I wanted the ground to open up and swallow me. I wanted to crawl away. I even wanted to die. Now another side of me flares up. The urge to fight, to stand up and scream so loud the building shakes, to go mad and harm everyone in the room indiscriminately. Both sides of me fight and my energy levels rise.

Thankfully, the fear is still there and strong, stopping me

from carrying out my murderous desires. I laugh at myself. I'm squirming around in fear with my heart having sunk to the floor and I think I want to stand up, scream and lash out violently. I know myself well enough to know that isn't me and I know that it won't solve a thing and will only give these interrogators more reason to punish me and more reason to believe Kris's lies. No, the balance between my fear and outright anger shows me a better and more calculated way. It is the truth that is needed here.

I start to let my mind root out the memories that my whole body has been fighting to keep locked away and secured. I squeeze my mother's hand a little tighter. I raise my gaze from the floor and look the lead Elder in the eyes and I start my journey:

I tell them about Kris's invitation one evening to have dinner with him and Julie.

"I thought it a little odd as I was kind of close to Julie, but I didn't really know Kris that well except for seeing him at the Kingdom Hall and occasionally witnessing on the streets with him. I had never spent time alone with him. I never spend any time alone with any male company as I have been brought up not to put myself and others in the way of sexual temptation.

"I was looking forward to seeing Julie. We always got on so well despite our age difference and I was excited about seeing her in her own environment, in her own home. It was a weeknight and I went straight there from school. It was a little further to travel than walking home, so took a while longer. It was the beginning of winter and it was cold and already getting darker as the nights began to get longer."

My brain starts to rush quicker than my mouth can tell the Elders what happened. Verbally I talk about the cold walk, in my head my memories are already in hell and I fight to carry on.

"When I got to Julie's house and knocked on the door, it was Kris that answered and let me in. Once inside the house I removed my shoes and Kris took my coat and hung it up. As I walked into the kitchen, I realised that no-one was there, so I asked where Julie was, and Kris said that she was a little late getting home."

"Why did you go inside the house first and then ask where Julie was?" asks one of the Elders.

"I didn't expect Julie not to be there. I was asked to go straight from school. I assumed that both of them would be in the house because I was on time as arranged."

"Were you happy that Julie wasn't there and that you were alone with Kris?" asks the other Elder in a patronising tone.

"I was extremely uncomfortable and very confused. Julie was supposed to be there. I didn't know what to do. I know I should have left straight away, and the thought did cross my mind, but Kris had taken my coat and shoes. He then started to laugh and joke with me and I became relaxed around him. He's a Ministerial Servant and I'm a schoolgirl. I wasn't particularly frightened of him, I didn't feel threatened, just a little awkward."

The lead Elder leans forward with a keen interest. "Why didn't you leave? You were uncomfortable. You knew it was wrong to be there on your own with a Brother in the congregation. You know about the lure of temptation to sin, so why did you stay in the house?"

"Because he insisted that Julie was going to be walking through the door at any minute. I had no reason to doubt him. It would have been very rude to insist on having my shoes and coat back and walk out the door." My voice raises slightly. Once again it seems that the questions being thrown at me are a lot more accusatory than inquisitive. I fight within, between having any of the energy I had built up being quashed and recoiling back into my shell and getting angrier and shouting at them. I feel so confused and conflicted. I just keep reminding myself that this evening will soon be over, this will finish and I will have faced my haunting fears.

The lead Elder leans back into his chair and one of the other Elders asks me to carry on.

"Kris then asked if I wanted a tour of the house as I had never been there before. I thought nothing of it. We have such a large congregation, there are many houses I have never been in and it always seems to be a custom to be shown around on a first visit. Besides it broke what I thought was an awkward and uncomfortable moment before Kris started joking around and offering me the tour. That's when he started touching me again, "that's when he…" I can't finish the sentence. My mind skips several details and mental pictures and hits me square in the head with a dreadful and horrifying image which my whole body rejects immediately. I can't help my reaction: my eyes start to fill up with tears, my body shakes, I can feel stabbing intense pain in my lower abdomen and my gaze falls to the floor almost by default.

I can't do it. I cannot relive it. I did everything I could to not be there when it happened, and I don't want to go back and pick up what I missed the first time around. There was a reason I went to that beach, there was a reason I looked deep into that beautiful blue sky, there was reason for escaping in any way I possibly could.

I can hear the lead Elder push forward onto the edge of his chair. Without looking at him I can feel his eyes watching me, I can sense the eagerness for detail and to push me where I do not want to go.

"Why did you follow him around the house? You knew you were alone together in the house. Were you hoping something might happen? Had you imagined something romantic happening between you and Kris before you even got to the house?"

His questions, although annoyingly accusatory once again, at least brought me back from that moment in my memory and rewound it to walking around the house. It feels like a short respite. I pick up my head slightly, my eyes still brimming with tears and I feel a meagre spike of energy. I deny all his questions. I explain that Julie was my friend and Kris was the husband of my friend. I try to explain that I just didn't see Kris in that way at all.

The respite doesn't last long.

"Can you go into more detail, where were you when you say he touched you? Where in the house where you?"

I can remember so vividly how it all started, those are the pieces I already have clearly in my memory and they alone are horrific enough not to want to relive them. I take a deep breath and start to explain.

"It started in the main bedroom. I went into the room first and Kris came up close behind me and started to touch my back and hair as he had done when we were on the ministry. It shocked me. At first, I didn't know what he was doing. I just stood still because I realised what was happening and how much more frightening it was because we were alone together in the house and in his bedroom. I knew it was wrong and I became very frightened. I thought about how it would look if Julie suddenly came into the room and how devastated she would be. It was only then that the realisation dawned on me that I was on my own and that was even more frightening. I didn't want to move and I hoped he would just walk away into the next room. It was then that he shoved me violently onto the bed."

"Stop there," the lead Elder breaks in. "So didn't you tell

him to stop?"

I can feel my mind teetering on the edge. The lead Elder stopped me at the horror moment when I had really started to play through and realise my worst fear coming to light in my memory. I feel like I am standing on the brink, looking over the edge of a huge cliff and just being held back from falling. I can't help but lower my head and gaze down to the floor, to my feet and the grubby industrial carpet. I can hardly see for the build-up of tears in my eyes. I want this to be over and done with and the Elders aren't letting me get on with it and get it finished. They seem intent on torturing me rather than getting information out of me.

I quietly try to explain how frozen I was in that bedroom, frightened of the situation and even more scared of where it was going. An intense and inner fear had taken over my body and I felt trapped and held in purgatory. Every explanation to the Elders seems to be met with scepticism and even more questions. I fluctuate between sinking low and down into the ground as I take another step closer to the place where every fibre in my being wants to escape from, to getting stopped and quizzed again and again for more detail. Every time we stop it makes me angry and picks me up out of my depressive slump and makes me want to fight back at them.

Were my clothes provocative? Did I do anything to encourage him? Was I aroused? Was he aroused? Did I tell him to stop? Every question is loaded with intent and a distinct undertone. I sense the course of this interrogation has already been mapped out beforehand. Each question is almost an accusation which just fuels my anger and gives me energy I know I wouldn't otherwise have.

So far, I have been as vague as possible on detail. We are already delving into memories I do not want to see and relive. Every vision in my head, every snapshot of memory, comes with a flurry of pain both physical and mental, the anguish and darkness so deep and frightening that I become fearful of my own reactions. I'm in a state I do not understand and the thought of the consequences of how I react to every look, every question, make me feel even more scared as though any control I may have is fleeting. I can feel a build-up of extreme anxiety and anger, the two battling each other for control over my body. I relish the thought of just letting rip and giving all control over to my anger. I also want to lose control to the depression and sink into the floor, pass out, slip into a coma, die even. Somewhere in the middle is my sense of duty, love for my mum and family, my upbringing to love God and respect his way, his organisation and his personally appointed Elders. Those feelings keep me in the centre and fighting for balance.

"He pushes me face down onto the bed very violently and jumps onto my back and rips at my clothes and rapes me on the bed where he sleeps with his wife." I forcefully spit out. That's all I need to say. It's all there. It's done and finished, and I feel a sense of relief that I have said it all.

I slump down into my chair feeling relieved. I haven't had to delve into my memories and I immediately start to think of the sand in my fingers, the warm air and the slight sting of hot sunshine on my skin. I recall the deep blue of the sky and it relaxes me. The more I think of the depth of that deepest blue, the more I can feel the pull towards it, and it feels like a warm blanket surrounding me and keeping me safe, dry and warm.

"So, did you scream?" a voice says breaking the calmness. "Did you shout out, did you protest?"

It's the lead Elder again, leaning forward and staring straight at me with malice and clear intention. His question stirs my mother into action. She moves forward, almost falling of her chair trying to put herself between the lead Elder and me.

"How is that relevant?!" My mum almost screams. "Hasn't she gone through enough already? When you have your face shoved into a mattress how are you going to scream?" she says pointing at the lead Elder.

One of the other Elders then starts to speak gently and opens his Bible and begins to direct my mum to read a passage from the Old Testament. For a moment I was drifting back into a passive state but the sudden bursts of anger and then another lull as they read passages from the Bible makes me uneasy once again and puts me straight into an internal battle all over again.

I feel sick. I hoped it was all over and for a moment it was and yet it still rages on. The other Elder explains the Bible passages about a woman who is guilty of adultery if she does not shout out, struggle and protest. I feel the stuffiness of archaic law starting to oppress me. We really do live in the dark ages! But then my questioning mind fights and tries to balance everything out. I start to internally question myself, the way the Elders are questioning. Did I give off any signals? Did I desire Kris subconsciously? Was I jealous of Julie? Did I scream, did I fight, did I say no?

As the discussion carried on the inevitable happened. Because I am sitting here questioning myself, my mind rushes at a thousand miles an hour for answers. I start to fold back up again and my head drops down all over again. Was there a moment where I wanted all that to happen? The question wakes the memories and the blue skies disappear. The sand falls from my fingers and in the palm of my hand I can feel cloth instead. As I pull my fingers into a very tight fist, I can feel the duvet inside my tightening grip.

Then, with a spike of unbearable pain, I feel blood, terror, horror and the darkness of death itself. Against every cell of my body, against every desire in my head, the real images of memory come flooding back into my mind. Everything I did not want to face and see the first time around come rushing into light. Once the floodgates open, I cannot stop it and I sit bolt upright and nearly throw up all over the lead Elder in front of me. Along with it comes a rush of the darkest anger and hate I have ever felt.

I sit, struggling to keep hold of the mental balance I had moments before. I look at the lead Elder who has been shocked back into his chair and I can see a glimpse of fear in his eyes. I feel possessed and I must look it as well judging by the reaction I'm getting.

Before the Elders get to say anything, I allow the anger to build in me, greater and greater. To my surprise, I still have control over it and in my head I see a clear plan. Do they want to know what really happened? Do they really want all the details, the whole story? Well the cat is out of the bag now and the floodgates are open. They are going to get everything!

Controlling the anger, the pain, the hurt, the horror and channelling it all into my mouth, I tell them everything. What Kris did to me. How he did it. How much it hurt. The damage he did to my body. The blood, the torn flesh, the smell, the tears. I threw it all at them. Raw and fresh as it ripped through my own recall. The intensity of my words physically knocks them back into their seats and they start to slump down in their chairs instead. Each moment I describe, gives me more anger and more energy and power as I explain in detail how Kris left me on the bed and disappeared. My mum looks at me in horror as I express the shame in detail, at how frightened I was that Kris would return and start the ordeal all over again before I could leave. I tell them all about the amount of blood that covered me as I eventually made my way out of the house and then spent two hours getting home. I told them how, thankfully, no-one was home and I managed to clean myself and wash my shame and evidence away in the shower. I then explained to them how it happened again when Kris visited our house on another two occasions.

My mum is beside herself in tears. In order to channel my anger at the Elders, my mum was also in range of the full truth. Something she obviously wasn't prepared for. My mum begins to apologise to me through a barrage of tears and hugs.

I feel an intense satisfaction and pride. I did it. I faced the demons head on. I must have looked half possessed. I was so angry with the way the Elders were talking to me that the whole truth was shot directly at them in angry and truthful detail. My mum and I hugged, and she got out her handkerchief and started to dab the tears from her face. The Elders just sat there in shock. The recollection of the events came so quick and fast in my mind and to deal with them I had forced them verbally out just as fast. It exorcised my fears, but it also made me live it all over again. As I spoke, I relived the pain inside mentally and physically. I can still feel those wounds, my torn flesh as though they had been ripped open anew. My stomach throbs and stabs. Such pain. As I involuntarily double over in my chair, pulling myself out from my mother's arms, the lead Elder sat forward again and spoke.

"I have to ask these questions; I hope you understand." He leans forward even more and puts his hand on my knee. "If you bled as much as you say, why hasn't your mother seen your bloodied clothes?"

The way he asked was so purposefully slow and once again accusatory. He is accusing me of lying, using that tone. He is not directly saying it, but that is the subtext in his use of those words. I cannot believe the way this has developed. All my hopes and strength had been used believing that the hit of truth in their face would leave them in no doubt as to Kris's guilt and my innocence. An innocence moments ago I was severely starting to question myself. Surely God wouldn't allow this to progress even further if I was truly innocent. What have I missed, what did I do, where did I go wrong? I explain to the Elders, now more quietly and less sure, the anger subsiding, how I collected my stained and ripped clothes and put them into a neighbour's dustbin.

"Why would you do that?" one of the other Elders speaks up.

I knew why. I didn't want anyone to know. I didn't want my family to know. I felt ashamed. I certainly wasn't sure how my father would react. It's likely for that reason that my mum hasn't involved my dad either so far. I don't want to be responsible for more hurt and violence. But I don't have the energy to explain any of that to the Elders. They have taken the wind from me. As I hold my stomach the pain intensifies. I roll forward in a slumped, depressed state on the chair, which I realise just invites further attack from my oppressors.

"If you were hurt, in pain and bleeding, didn't you go to the hospital? Maybe we could call the hospital and verify your visit?" Those words could be taken as concerning if read from a book, but the delivery was far from that. There is a firm basis for accusation in these questions. It's clear that Kris is not on trial here – I am.

I couldn't go to the hospital; I knew that doing so risked more exposure. For a week I was in absolute agony, fearful that permanent damage had been done and that there was a possibility that my wounds were infected. I feared that I could die. I had isolated myself in my bedroom for a whole week under the cover of a stomach bug. My mum was concerned enough to try and persuade me to go to the doctors, but I refused and purposefully played it down.

But now I don't say anything to the Elders. My energy levels are falling, as is my desire to fight. My head drops further and once again I'm staring at the carpet below me.

"Did anyone witness this attack, do you know? Did anyone see you in this bloodied state? Did anyone see you put the bloodied clothes in the neighbour's waste bin?" All three of them now ask questions, one after the other. There seems to be either accusation or purpose behind all of them. I don't understand why those questions seemed so pointed. The lead Elder once again presses forward.

"We have to take our direction from Jehovah and from his organisation and we are clearly instructed as to when we can take action and when we cannot," he says, while once again opening his Bible. We Elders have clear instruction to follow, please look through this Bible passage with me."

He then goes on to read again from the Old Testament about how two witnesses are needed to prove an accusation against someone.

"What?" my mother cries loudly, "how can that ever work? Rapists and paedophiles don't advertise up front for an audience! That's the most stupid thing I have ever heard!" Her voice is so loud I can hear the echo bounce back from the larger hall on the other side of the door. Her energetic outburst, filled with the same anger and energy I had just moments before, fills me with a glimmer of hope and stops my slide down to the floor beneath me. I feel so much pride and love for my mother, so much so that I feel an urge to stand up next to her and shout "Go mum!"

But I don't. I partially look up to see the lead Elder raise and show the palms of his hands towards my mother.

"Please calm down. These are God's rules, set out in the Bible clearly for our direction. These are wise and perfect rules for us all to live by. The Governing Body helps us maintain these laws in proceedings such as these. If you question the Bible and the rules of Jehovah's organisation, you put yourself in danger. That is apostasy that you speak. I know you are angry – that is understandable – but be careful what you say in anger because it can have severe repercussions."

My poor mother. The fight is instantly taken from her with just a few softly spoken words. She sits back down into her chair and turns her attention back to me again. I know what the Elders are implying to my mum in a not so subtle way. They are directly threatening her. If she goes against the Elders, she will be disfellowshipped herself. Thrown out from the Congregation. Humiliated and shunned from the whole world she knows, including her family, who will be told to have nothing to do with her even in her own home. The Elders killed my energy and now they have taken the wind from my mother's sails as well.

The room sinks into a disturbed quiet, only the whir of the electric fan heater breaking the silence.

It seems like an age before anyone speaks.

The room is still cold despite the little heater working overtime. I feel like I'm held in suspended animation. I'm exhausted from my outburst. My mum is noticeably wounded. The pain in my abdomen adds to the nausea I already feel. I've stopped sinking down towards the floor and yet I don't feel I have the energy or any desire to lift my head. I stay paralysed in a hunched position nursing my stomach pains with my mother's arm around me.

"We have just one more question before we take a break. Have you told any of this to the Police? Have you reported this?"

I shake my head and whisper, "No," keeping my eyes to the floor.

The Elders stand up and ask my mum and myself to go into the main hall and wait while they talk amongst themselves privately. The two of us lift ourselves up off the chairs and lean heavily on each other for support. We are both mentally and physically exhausted and we would both collapse without the support of the other.

We shuffle ourselves towards the door and one of the other Elders holds the door open for us. As we walk through into the main hall, the cold air hits me and refreshes me. I hadn't really noticed the tears on my face before the cold makes it obvious. The coolness helps ease my anxiety a little and takes away some of the abdominal pain I'm suffering. We both walk across the main hall which is dark except for one light at the end of the room. We move a couple of chairs around and sit as close as we can to each other as the door to the small room shuts behind us taking half the light of the hall with it. Then there is silence.

My mum puts her arms around me and squeezes me so tightly. I'm so relieved that it's all over, that I did what my mother guided me to do and faced the terror and relived it all for a second time. Despite that small relief, in my memory I had opened Pandora's Box. Those images, the memory of the pain, the darkness and depression I had tried so very hard to hide is now fresh and open. Not like an open wound, but more like an amputation. A large part of my innocent self is gone leaving me open and in pain. I know I will never be the same again and I know my relationship with my mother will never be the same either.

My mum pulls away from our embrace and looks me in the eyes.

"You have been so brave my beautiful daughter and I am so very, very sorry that I let this happen to you. I'm supposed to protect my child and I have failed in the worst possible way. I will never forgive myself. I hope you can forgive me. I love you so much."

Tears run down her face. I can see the sadness and shame in her eyes. It is a genuine heartfelt plea that I didn't think was necessary. Then her face changes slightly and she holds my shoulders firmly and looks at me intensely. "No matter what they say in that room, from here on, I will NEVER let you down again. Nothing they say to us in that room will change anything between us and I will always love my daughter with all my heart. I am with you."

I'm so confused. Surely, I have been through the worst. What does my mother know that I am not seeing? I have done everything the Elders have asked. I have put my faith in Jehovah and told the truth, even explicitly as they asked. I want it all to be finished. I want it all to be tidied away and let me get on with my life and start to heal if that is at all possible.

My mind starts to wander. What do I think should happen to Kris? I honestly don't know. There is a part of me that hates him intensely with so much anger that his death might be the only fitting judgement. I feel so bad, so guilty for thinking that way. I know that's not God's way, that's not the Christian way to think. What kind of a human being am I to think that way? But then he has taken so much from me, so much that I don't know if I can survive this. I have so many dark thoughts. Thoughts of anger and violence against myself, against Kris, against the Elders, against God. I am losing my spiritual soul and I don't know if I can survive without it.

I hope the Elders don't ask me what I think should be done with Kris. I just want to be left alone now. I have done the difficult bit. I want to go home with my mother and stay away from the rest of the world. But I know that cannot happen no matter how much I wish for it.

I start to think about whether my life can have any normality now. I know I had to go through this trial, but no part of me had wondered about life on the other side of it. How do I go on, how do I behave? Who am I anymore?

I begin to panic deep inside myself. If I don't know who I am, how on earth am I meant to act? I've never bothered to take any real notice of myself before, I've never self-analysed to any real extent. What makes up me? How do I walk? Do I have a way of walking, do I have a swagger? How do I hold myself, do I have any flair, or do I walk like a robot? I really don't want anyone to be suspicious that anything has happened to me. So how do I act the same way when I have no real idea of how I act and look to other people in order to maintain the illusion of normality? I'm in the Kingdom Hall right now. Tomorrow it will be packed with a hundred people all looking at me and yet I have no clue who I am anymore. I suppose that acting up, playing the carefree flirt is just easier. It's a character that I can play and enjoy being without having to think about being truly seen. A character can be analysed as much as I allow it because the mask cannot be penetrated.

I start to feel sick all over again. The uncertainty is sending me in a spin and my anxiety hits the roof. The thought of returning to normal life is enough to worry about. Wondering what is being discussed behind that door is even worse.

My mother and I sit in a silent embrace. There is a pattering sound against the window through the darkness outside. It has started to rain again. It' is cold inside the main hall, so much so that I can see my breath in the air. Why is it that fear has a greater hold when in the cold? When you are warm, fear seems less of a monster. Maybe it's the shared shivering that adds a dimension. I want the Elders to hurry up and finish this. It seems that after every hurdle I am faced with there is yet another one to overcome. I sit hoping that returning to that room will be the last hurdle.

I stare at the door hoping that it will open soon while I have some strength left in me to go through it and face the final challenge if, of course, it's going to be the final, final challenge. I can see light framing the door into the smaller room and I can still smell the faint stale burning of the fan heater. We can barely make out human voices, muffled and mumbling from within. My mum looks at me with concern and heartache. Poor mum.

I can hear footsteps and shuffling from within the room and then the door opens, casting a beam of light across the main hall. This is it. The anxiety lifts me again to another level and I try to stand up from the chair, but my legs fail beneath me and I fall back down into it, nearly falling off the chair entirely. My mum rushes to grab me and stabilises me, then helps me back to my feet. I am so fearful that my feet don't want to move and take me to this final destination. I feel as though this is the march of death, a last moment before my body is left soulless and devoid of spirituality.

The Elder at the door asks the two of us to go back into the room and we slowly make our way back through the door into the small, stale-smelling room. I keep on saying to myself that I am nearly there, that the descent is almost complete, that I need to hang on just a little while longer. The Elder shuts the door behind us and we take our places again on the plastic chairs. My head immediately goes straight down to the floor, to my feet below me. I take one quick glance at the panel of three. The lead Elder is sitting upright, so very sure of himself, pointed and direct. The Elder to the left looks me straight in the eyes, but sits back, obviously subservient to the lead Elder. I think to myself "They are supposed to be equal," but the body language in front of me says differently. The Elder on the right, the one that invited us both back into the room, cannot make eye contact with me. He looks away from my gaze and looks to be in some discomfort. I can imagine a very telling photograph of the three of them in a gallery, so much to glean from one captured image.

The lead Elder clears his throat and begins to speak. "We have gathered all the information together. We have taken in what you have told us. We have spoken to Kris at length yesterday. We have prayed to Jehovah for guidance and we have sought wisdom from Bethel and brought all that together. We are all unanimous in our judgement." With that he asks us to open our Bibles and he reads a couple of scriptures. I can't concentrate and my brain goes into whirlwinds of thoughts and scenarios as well as horrific flashing images of my many ordeals. The floodgates have opened, and I'm paralysed by their imagery. So much so that I do not hear what the scripture is, what it is about and where they are going with their conversation. I am so lost in my thoughts that the one word I do pick out throws me straight back into the room with a shocking clatter.

"Disfellowshipped!"

Catching that one word makes me jump and I have no idea of its context. I'm stunned back into the here and now and reeling from the word. I'm trying frantically to work out who they are talking about. Is it Kris? Have they made the wise decision and finally seen him for what he is? The possibility lifts me from my slumber, it spikes energy back into my tired and aching body. I sit upright in my chair and look over to my mother with a mixture of a half-smile and total confusion.

The returned look is not what I expect. Tears are forming in my mother's eyes. She looks at me with pity and sadness and she puts her arm around me as I look back to the Elders with puzzlement.

"We don't take this decision lightly at all, but you leave us with little choice in light of your conduct." I look to the Elder on the right and he looks away back towards the door we came in through.

"You clearly admit to fornication," says the lead Elder "We just cannot work out with whom. We know it's not Kris. Apart from the fact that he is a fine brother, a trusted and hardworking Ministerial Servant and a happily married man, he was also somewhere else, specifically on the first day you described."

I struggle to comprehend where this is all leading. I'm so confused as to who is disfellowshipped if they are talking about Kris so positively. My thoughts go into hyperdrive and spin all over the place. My head starts to feel dizzy and I hold on to mother's arm to stabilise myself.

"You obviously have an issue with Kris, a jealousy of Julie perhaps, I don't know. But these are serious accusations you have made. It's obvious you had sex with someone. The fact that you are unwilling to tell the truth just shows your lack of repentance and the level of your insincerity. Your recent behaviour and the sheer level of these lies and stories that frankly, are hideous and have no foundation or evidence in fact, lead us to think that you are manipulative and attention-seeking. There's not even a second witness to these accusations which just makes the whole situation worse.

"You have put us all in a situation where we just cannot afford to compromise. You bring shame to the congregation; you bring shame to your family; and you bring shame to Jehovah's name and that cannot be tolerated and must be dealt with harshly and swiftly."

I'm the one being disfellowshipped? I am being shamed and thrown out?

I struggle to comprehend how on earth they managed to make it solely my fault, how they cannot see Kris for what he is and what he has done, and how I have ended up being punished so harshly for being abused, damaged and hurt.

As my mind tries to work out what this all means, the Elders carry on talking into the background and out of my direct attention once again. I'm in absolute shock. I have seen disfellowshipped people in the congregation and I know exactly how they are treated. No-one in the congregation, if fact none of Jehovah's Witnesses are allowed to acknowledge them, talk to them, help them or have anything to do with them whatsoever until the time that the Elders have decided that they are repentant enough to be allowed back into the congregation. Even when accepted back in, for decades they can be outcasts and viewed as damaged goods. People in the congregation stay clear of people formerly disfellowshipped as though they are proven to be prone to wickedness.

As a disfellowshipped person, all my friends will have to ignore me, for months. I don't have any friends from school as I'm not really allowed to associate with people outside of the Kingdom Hall, even kids I know and see every day. My family will be told to keep association with me to a minimum. How on earth do we do that? The past few months I have felt isolated enough as it is, now I really will be on my own.

Oh no. Then of course there's the whole humiliation of it all. I've seen this play out at the Kingdom Hall, and it seems so unfair. At every event, a disfellowshipped person can only turn up at the Kingdom Hall when everything has started, so they don't embarrass anyone there by forcing them to ignore a former friend and colleague. The disfellowshipped person must leave just before the end of the meeting, again so they don't accidently interact with anyone. They must sit at the back of the Kingdom Hall on their own, isolated like someone diseased. And they must do that for months, to show and prove that they are sincere about being allowed back into the congregation. I will have to go through all of that. That process will also bring shame on my whole family as well because I won't be able to sit with them at the Kingdom Hall. Of course, everyone will know that I belong to the family that are sitting at the other end of the hall. I will be reminding everyone at the Kingdom Hall twice a week that my family shares my disgrace.

If that wasn't embarrassing enough, there would be the disciplinary talk as well. Yet another cringe-worthy, awful and humiliating experience. First there will be an announcement from the platform in front of the whole congregation. I will be named, and everyone will be told that I am disfellowshipped, so that everyone from that point on would know that they would have to treat me differently. I would have to sit through that and so would my poor family and friends. Then a few weeks after that, supposedly at a random time, a special lecture from the platform will be performed by one of these three Elders, giving guidance to the congregation about the subject matter for which I am being punished. This has always been to make sure that the congregation are clear as to what the boundaries are over a specific sin. For everyone in the congregation, it is always the confirmation of what someone has been punished for. It's not supposed to be. The talk is supposed to be held at a random time after the event, but everyone always puts the two together so very easily. Someone gets publicly punished one week, and then a month or so later a random talk on a specific subject gives everyone the opportunity to put it all together.

That process really will be the ultimate embarrassment. What would the Elder talk about? What specifically is my crime? The more I think about it the worse that scenario gets in my head. Surely, they aren't accusing me of making up being sexually attacked. They are, aren't they? And they are saying that I didn't struggle or scream which makes me complicit. The horror of that. If those are their accusations, will they be the subject matter of that "random" talk in a month or so's time? I cannot sit through that. Not in front of the congregation. Not in front of my family. Not in front of my friends. Not in front of Julie.

I can't breathe. All of this is just too much. I must be a truly wicked person to have got to this place. What kind of evil must I be for Jehovah to directly accuse me of such atrocities? I cannot help but question my own sanity. Have I really done everything they are saying? These are Elders. Older and wiser people that are appointed by God. We have done all this under God's guidance and in his presence at the Kingdom Hall under the guidance of prayer and scripture. But it all feels so wrong and out of place. I am so confused.

We all stand to our feet. I have no idea what has been said in the last ten minutes as my mind and heart are sinking so fast and I have no idea who I am anymore. I'm so exhausted. I had built up all my energy to be able to see out this day and to get to this point when it would all be over, and yet I don't feel any relief at all. In fact, I feel like I am at the very beginning of a journey instead of being thankful to be at the end of one.

My mum has a firm hold of me as we shuffle our way out of the fusty room and back out into the cold large main hall. Only the quieter Elder follows us out and he softly tells my mum that should she need anything he will be there for support. I can hear the other two Elders casually talking to each other still in the small room and I'm surprised at their temperament. I cannot hear the words they are saying, but there isn't any melancholy or quiet about their tone, as though it was just another casual and cold evening at the Kingdom Hall.

I walk with my head down, leaning heavily on my mother who doesn't say a word. We exit the building and make our way through the cold and the rain across the car park and into the car. My mum takes me around the car and into the passenger side, opens the door for me and helps me into the seat of the car. I feel so blank, so confused, so dark and cold and so very empty. I must look like a barely walking corpse as I slump into the passenger seat of the car. My mum runs around the car, gets into the driver's seat and starts the engine in a rush and a panic. She is clearly flustered as she impatiently drives quickly out of the car park and onto the road. Through the window of the car, I can see the main door to the Kingdom Hall being closed from within, shutting us out. The dim lights of the hall barely shine out of the narrow high windows illuminating the rain.

"Don't you worry my brave girl," says my mother in a half

angry and half panicked state. "I think we have to get your dad involved now. There is no way I'm turning my back on my beautiful and brave daughter. Don't you worry, there is no way we are shunning you. You have done absolutely nothing wrong, do you hear me? This whole thing stinks. It's immoral!" She reaches over to me with one hand on the steering wheel, still driving in a mad rush panic and grabs my hand. "I love you. We are not going to treat you like a disfellowshipped person. This is all wrong. I love you my baby."

5 - HOPE

It's been two months since I was last at the Kingdom Hall that night in the cold and wet and now we are here again. The last two months have been such a turmoil and it seems to just continue without end. My life feels like I'm riding a rollercoaster, constantly going up and down, being buffeted left to right. Sometimes I have no idea which way I'm facing or where I'm going. I seem to have no control over my own life or destiny.

Although we are once again meetings Elders in private at the Kingdom Hall, this time both my mum and dad are with me and I at least feel so supported, believed and comforted by their presence. It still doesn't change the fact that, once again, I am here. It also doesn't help that perhaps the situation has picked up its own momentum where I feel totally without any say or control over what is happening. I love my parents so much and they have stuck by me with so much love and comfort through all of this, but they have also been the driving force in getting us all here, when perhaps I would have preferred to have just left everything alone and quietly sunk into a dark corner somewhere.

Our car pulls into the car park and we all get out. At least this time it's not raining and the air feels a little warmer than before, although it's still chilly. There is a great difference this time to both the previous occasions. I still feel extremely apprehensive, but I don't feel as though this is the possible end to my life. So much has happened over the past two months.

As we all walk to the main entrance to the Hall, the door swings open from the inside and two Elders come out to meet us with handshakes, smiles and kisses. There is a noticeable and uncomfortable hesitance when they interact with me though when compared to the greeting with my parents. But it is an understandable discomfort, which is on my part as well. We all know that neither of these two Elders or myself should be meeting and greeting like this as I am shamed and disfellowshipped. The fact that we interact at all is a minor miracle, especially after all that isolation.

When we left the Kingdom Hall that cold rainy night two months ago, I thought my life had ended. The only glimmer of hope and any warmth in a completely cold and dark world was the lifeline my mother held out to me. When we got home that night, I sobbed for an hour in my mother's arms. I then drifted into a haunted and desolately lonely sleep with the sound of my parents muffled discussion taking place downstairs.

I don't know what my father's initial reaction that night was. They must have talked well into the morning hours because none of the family awoke until very late the next morning. It was a Saturday morning and when we met in the kitchen, we all embraced as a family. Then my father took us all out for the day shopping, bowling and a meal out in the evening. It was such a perfect day after the deepest low in my life. My dad was wonderful and hardly stopped cuddling me, holding me and telling me how much he loved me. I felt quite bad that I just didn't want the attention and kept shrugging him off all day, but he never stopped and inside it did make me feel loved and comforted, even though I refused to show it.

On the Sunday, we should have gone on the preaching work and then to the Kingdom Hall, but instead my dad took us all to the seaside for the day. It was cold and extremely unusual to not go to the meeting on a Sunday and that did feel very strange. I couldn't help but feel a little guilty that I was perhaps pulling my family away from the Kingdom Hall. Both my parents that day said that it was just a one-off and I was not to read anything into it. As far as they were concerned it was a desperately needed family day. The whole weekend was almost perfect except for the obvious unnerving sentence that now weighted above my head and was set to bring reproach and shame to this family I love so much.

I was grateful that we didn't go the Kingdom Hall that Sunday. I didn't know how I would face it. The situation would have been so creepy, upsetting and very uncomfortable. Not to mention awkward beyond measure. Nothing had been announced to the congregation at that point as there hadn't been a meeting since my judgement was passed. Announcements were never made on a Sunday anyway; they were always made on a Thursday evening. Nobody would have known that I was disfellowshipped. It would have been very confusing as to how I should act on that Sunday. It would have been so very wrong, knowing I was disfellowshipped, to go and seek one last opportunity to spend close time with my friends and non-immediate family before they knew of my punishment. I would have needed to have kept my distance from all of them. Someone would have noticed and asked why I was being distant. It would also have been seen as wrong to have told everyone myself before the announcement. One of the many unwritten rules of being a Jehovah's Witness.

Both my parents told me that life at home was not going to change at all. That worried me because I knew they would eventually get into trouble themselves if they did that. Although I enjoyed that weekend so much, I worried a lot about bringing more trouble into the family because of my actions. I had been in the deepest depression for months. It built its way down deeper to another low point at those Elders' judicial meetings. It was an experience I never wanted to relive. To spend such a lovely weekend with my family and to be so close to them was a slight pull up out of that trench that I was once again at the bottom of.

After that weekend, my parents sat me down and explained what they were going to do. They decided that for me to be forced to go into the Kingdom Hall and not only face the congregation under the shame of being disfellowshipped but also be forced to see Kris twice a week, would be the worst hell to put me through. They also made sure to tell me that they believed everything I had told the Elders about what Kris had done to me.

I couldn't believe they said that to me, and we all together cried for what seemed like ages – even my dad whom I had never seen cry before. It was horrible to sit with them telling me all those things. I felt something very strange happening within me. When all this started, I felt so very isolated and alone. Kris took away my entire world. I was left with no-one at all. I was never sure how my parents would react and what the consequences might have been. I was in complete isolation. Only when my mother knew the whole truth did I start to feel a glimmer of light against the darkness of loneliness. I was battling against having to relive the full horror of my experience and then being called a liar by the Elders. One experience pushed me down while my mother tried to throw me a single lifeline in all the despair.

Having my father know also brought a mixed bag of feelings. I did not want him to know. I knew that he couldn't understand. I thought he might have been angry at me, especially having now been disfellowshipped. I have brought so much dishonour to the family. If he did believe me, I wasn't sure how he would react, what he might do to Kris. It is all my shame and, as such, I don't want anyone to know. I couldn't help but feel betrayed by my mum in a way that she had told him my darkest secret. I trusted my mother to be my keeper of secrets. But I suppose everything was about to fall apart around us and my father deserved to know the reason why. All these mixed up emotions made me doubt my mum for a while. And yet, through all that regret, I had another ally, another person that loved me and made me feel less alone and with every step came a greater sense of hope, even though the hope was still very slight and delicate.

When both my parents sat me down, they said to me that I had been so very brave, but they wanted me to be brave again. They were both convinced that Kris had very likely done the same thing to other young people and could still be doing it others in the congregation even now. They felt a responsibility to expose Kris and to help those other poor young children. They told me explicitly that it would be a painful journey for me if they tried to expose what was happening in the congregation, but the choice was mine. If I didn't want to do anything more, they would respect that decision.

I had never for a moment thought about that at all. I was so grateful that at least my ordeal was finished and that I wouldn't ever have to go through that again, that it never occurred to me that Kris might have other young people that he was victimising. When they said that to me, I was confused and pulled apart. I was so relieved that the worst was hopefully behind me. I was in hope that I could try my best to hide away and never have to face that experience again. If it is true that I was so brave, then I wanted to have a free life for what I had earned and to be left alone.

I felt very selfish thinking that way. The more I thought about it, the worse I felt inside. I couldn't help but think about the possibility of someone else in the congregation being put through what I had gone through. I thought about my friends and if any of those had been anywhere near Kris. I started to have nightmares about seeing Kris touching children at the Kingdom Hall and those thoughts started to dominate my day to day thinking. I became torn between being tired of struggle and shame and finding that growing anger and rebellion in me again. Part of me wanted proper justice and another part of me thought that the whole congregation deserved everything they get for the way I had been treated. I also wondered why I shouldn't think like that, I was the one that had to suffer.

It was only a few days of self-agony and torture until I went back to my parents and agreed with them that there might be other victims and we had to help them too, by stopping Kris. In one way that was a relief to stop my mind consuming itself with guilt, but it also meant the reality of facing this demon once again and going through another process of pain and suffering. I also realised that even if I decided not to agree with my parents and pursue justice, I was still facing the horror that goes with being disfellowshipped. I was going to suffer regardless; it may as well be worthwhile.

Both my parents were so very proud of me making that decision. Their first choice was to immediately stop attending the congregation that we were a part of. We had a bit of a blessing really in that the Kingdom Hall building was used by two congregations. The two never really met as they used the Hall at completely different times. So, that week we started to meet with the other congregation. The announcement that I was being disfellowshipped was on the Thursday. None of us would be there to face it, which would get the family into some trouble. My father said he would have to work fast to get things in motion as the Elders would likely come and visit my mum and dad at our home straight after the meeting on seeing that they weren't there.

My dad got in touch with the Elders in the new congregation, told them what had happened with me and that really the Police should be informed what Kris had done to me. The three Elders my dad talked to at the new congregation are called Alan, Bob and John. My dad knew all of them from when the two congregations were one many years ago. My dad says that Alan, Bob and John were all appalled by the treatment I had received, not just by Kris, but also by the Elders in the other congregation. Although they had to respect the decision that those three Elders had made and would have to abide by it for a while, Alan, Bob and John would find out how to officially go about reporting the matter to the Police in a responsible way. So, they promised my dad that they would get in touch with the main Jehovah's Witnesses branch office in the country and get advice on how to proceed.

So that Friday, as a Family we sat in the new congregation and basically took our medicine knowing that matters had been set in motion. I sat there on that Friday knowing that all my friends and the rest of the family had been in the same Kingdom Hall the night before listening to the announcement that I had been disfellowshipped. I could imagine the gasps and tutting that most likely went around the hall that evening as well as the rush to talk to my relatives afterwards to try and glean as much gossip as possible. I could also imagine the filthy grin on Kris's face, a thought that filled me with so much anger. My family wasn't spared of course because the same announcement was made on the Friday night in the new congregation, but at least most people didn't know who I was. Although my dad knew a few people from a long time ago, I didn't know anyone at all, even though we all shared the same Hall. We all still had to come in late and sit at the back. My dad still talked to some people after the meeting. It could all have been so much worse than it was.

This was to be our new life now. I was to walk in shame in the presence of strangers, strangers that were not allowed to talk to me. All my friends had gone. All my non-immediate family were gone. It would seem as though in order to build up from my total isolation, I must rebuild one person at a time and lose everyone else in the process. I am grateful to have my family, a family that love me enough to ignore what they have been told to do and follow their hearts. I must be grateful for that.

So here we are, once again meeting one evening with Elders in the Kingdom Hall. Only this time we are meeting Alan, Bob and John, Elders from the new congregation. The Kingdom Hall doesn't seem as cold as two months ago. Maybe it's the weather that has changed or maybe it's the welcome. The Hall is the same as before; cold, fusty and empty. Cheerful banter is exchanged between my dad and Alan as Alan guides us through the main hall and into the small room at the back. We are welcomed by a boiled kettle and drinks are brewed and poured for everyone.

The atmosphere is totally different to before. I feel welcome and safer, but I put that down to the fact that I am not here to be disciplined. But then originally, I wasn't the first time. The mood is so different. I feel overwhelmed by kindness before anything is said. We are all invited to sit down on the plastic chairs. The chairs are laid out in a circle rather than in opposing lines. I sit next to my mother, but the Elders split themselves up with my dad.

After greetings are exchanged, John takes the lead. First, he directs everyone to join him in a prayer and that makes me nervous because it's the first time I see a similar pattern to the last judicial hearing. He then gets my dad and my mum to read a couple of Bible passages picked by the Elders and my body starts to go into shock because I realise, I have been through this all before. But then that's where the similarities end. John then starts to talk to us all.

"Thank you all so much for showing an extreme amount of patience and faith in Jehovah and in the three of us to look into this issue. I hope that Alan and Bob don't mind me saying that we think you have shown great faith and great courage to stay put and deal with the consequences of being disfellowshipped and the discomfort that brings with it. We don't take that sacrifice lightly.

"So, first of all, I'll take you through what has happened so far and where we are and then Bob can take you through the next steps, if that's ok?

"We didn't want you to have to go through the trauma of going through your experience all over again. After just a small amount of research it was clear that having to relive the pain and suffering of recalling your experience is just as traumatic as the experience itself and so should be repeated as few times as possible. In light of that we have tried to get your records from your old congregation and the original judicial hearing. At the same time, we have been in contact with both the circuit overseer and the main branch in the capital asking for advice about a second hearing and guidance on how to approach the police."

My mum begins to squeeze my hand and moves her other hand over so that both are holding me. It seems like they have done so much already. They speak with such more warmth and kindness, more than I have been used to, so much so that I can't help but start to fill up with tears as my mother squeezes my hand. Once again, my isolation bubble, which has been static for two months feels as though it just might expand slightly. As usual though I sense that it may come at a price, as the thought of being involved with the Police makes me so nervous and withdrawn once again.

John lets out a big sigh, which takes me by surprise.

"But we have had problems on every front. The Elders that took your judicial hearing are refusing to release their notes to us. The branch has told us that under no circumstances are we to take the matter to the Police until a further hearing involving both sets of Elders and the Circuit Overseer has taken place. This is a blow, but we must trust in Jehovah here and do the right thing.

"We are a little confused to tell you the truth because

these accusations are a matter of legality and breaking the law of the land. The Police have the right tools and expertise to investigate this kind of matter and we don't. I feel like a man being asked to repair a delicate computer with a sledgehammer, I just don't think we are professionally equipped to investigate something as serious as this. Besides which, I think there are some crossed wires here as well with the Circuit Overseer. The matter of law being broken is a matter for the Police, I think all of us here agree with that, whereas a Judicial Committee is a tool for ascertaining someone's spiritual crimes, not physical, not lawful. It is spiritual crimes against Jehovah's congregation that we are equipped to deal with not legal ones. There seems to be more emphasis on making sure public reproach is not brought against the organisation than doing the right thing morally.

"So that is the reason we are going to have this meeting with both Judicial Committees and the Circuit Overseer and try and get the right thing done. And if we do the right thing morally then Jehovah will bless us and make sure the wrongs are put right."

Alan jumps in "We can only apologise that nothing has been done and you might be justified in thinking that everyone is just stalling for time and hoping that you will just give up in exasperation. We will all meet together again in a couple of weeks, so we hope to have some more news for you just after that. Please carry on showing the extraordinary strength you have been, and we will reward the incredible patience you have shown by fighting your corner."

"There is also another reason that things have taken so long," Bob interrupts suddenly.

John gives Bob the dirtiest look. My dad notices and jumps straight in asking Bob to elaborate. Bob looks at John and shrugs his shoulders which just seems to open the conversation up. My dad starts to express to John that in order to have faith that the Elders have our interest at heart and to help us keep trust in them and their moral code, total honesty must be maintained. John replies reluctantly:

"We should not be talking about facts we do not know the full truth about, nor should we be expanding on inuendo and hearsay..." John looks straight at Bob with raised eyebrows and directed accusation, then looks back to me, "but you earned the right to know everything that is happening. This however must be kept confidential for now."

All of us have our interest piqued and all lean forward to catch what could possibly be of such intense interest. John sits back, takes a deep breath and says:

"Kris has several other investigations in both congregations being brought forward. It looks as though you were not on your own in your suffering."

I have an unexpected mix of feelings. I'm being taken a lot more seriously and just maybe even marginally justified in dragging my family through the rotten hell of the past few weeks. I also feel deeply sickened when suddenly realising that other young people have suffered at the hands of that filthy monster. But once again my world feels as though it is opening just slightly once again. My loneliness eases just that little bit.

We leave in agreement to get together again in a few short weeks. I sense a bit of rebellion between the two congregations and I'm stuck in the middle. Once again as light starts to shine just a little bit, clouds still gather, and thunder still roars close by. It seems that nothing can progress without a huge fight and battle to see the right thing being done. This is not what I have always thought God's organisation was about. I thought Jehovah's society was here to protect people like me. But then maybe Alan, Bob and John are going to fully restore my faith and help me see that it wasn't a mistake getting baptised and making a promise to God.

My mum, dad and I leave the Kingdom Hall, not happy, but at least with a minimum of a smile on our faces and a belief at least in the humanity of a few. There is the slightest of hopes that just maybe some justice may be done. That does carry the weight of responsibility though, and the sense of the beginning of a very long and terrifying journey. With both my parents on my side though I feel some strength to go   forward.

.

6 - REMAIN

Another four weeks have passed and yet again I am waiting outside the Kingdom Hall in a car. It appears my change into adult life is going to be defined by the act of visiting the Kingdom Hall to meet Elders outside of public meeting hours. The marginal euphoria I felt when we all left the hall four weeks ago passed quickly as the reality of everyday life as a disfellowshipped person kicked into play just hours after leaving.

Every day is a reminder of guilt and sin. I don't see any of my friends. I was so close to many of them and yet they all now ignore me. I understand sometimes, and yet other times I'm appalled by their behaviour. My friends should know me intimately and know whether I'm a bad person or not. It's hard not to be mad at them for being unable to work out what the trouble is and why I've been shamed, reprimanded and branded as bad company. But then, at the same time, although we live in such a close society where innuendo and gossip are rife, real secrets rarely surface. When rumour is king and truth becomes scarce under the faith that Jehovah will expose guilt and lies, it is easy to get trapped in the fast-moving river of whispers, political opinion and internal thought trend.

I also know that when the Elders say you do something,

you do it. I have been banished and everyone has been told to turn their back on me as an act of love. If the banishment hurts, then I will more likely fight to get back into the "spiritual family". I can't always be angry at my friends because it's very likely I would do the same if I was in their shoes.

Then, of course, there's the extended family. Nobody visits the family home anymore because I live there. My mum and dad are constantly getting a barrage of questions from the rest of the family. Why are they in a different congregation, why are they running away and not facing the punishment, why are they not shunning their daughter because in the end they will regret not doing it? My grandparents phone all the time and argue with my parents constantly. It makes me sad and ashamed because I am the cause of it all. My mum regularly sits me down and tells me that all this is not my fault. None of it occurred until my mum worked something out, which was based on me playing up. The playing up was a subconscious effort to gain attention, I see that now. So that still makes it my doing. I was still the catalyst for change.

There are some things that I don't miss. I cannot go preaching from door to door or stand in the street with a cart. I always hated doing any of that. I wasn't any good at it anyway. It's a relief as well not to be sent out with Kris.

We wait in the car outside the Kingdom Hall for the Elders to arrive. For once we are early. We always used to be early for the meetings twice a week. That has altered now that I'm disfellowshipped. I have to go into the Kingdom Hall after proceedings have started and must leave before they end. The whole family all go in together which I think is really kind of my mum and dad. Sometimes my dad hangs around for ten minutes at the end while my mum and I wait in the car, just so he can talk to a few people. It's the only time my parents see family, so my dad has to sort some matters out occasionally. I really couldn't have wished for better parents. I am so lucky.

Alan arrives in his car first. He parks up then opens the Kingdom Hall for us all to go inside. Although the weather is a little warmer, there are thunderclouds brewing and we can see a storm on its way from the east. I didn't fancy my mood getting much better if we got stuck in the car in a deluge. Although I'm still very anxious, the routine of these visits lessen the trepidation about what might come. I'm starting to realise that I cannot change or predict anything when it comes to talking to Elders.

As we enter the Hall, Bob and John drive in, park up and scurry in quickly behind us into the building. It doesn't take long to settle into the small back room and sit in our circle once again. My dad shakes hands with each Elder and they are all comfortingly casual and chirpy until we then go through the ritual of prayer and reading a Bible passage.

Passed that formality, Bob asks me how I am and how I'm coping with being under the restriction of being disfellowshipped. My anxiety has lifted since coming back into this small room again and I mumble quietly that I am coping ok. It doesn't seem appropriate to fix on my struggle with loneliness, depression, pain and the self-questioning of the strength and purpose of my faith.

Alan goes through a review up until when we last met four weeks ago. The recollection sobers the mood right down to a very serious point as my parents and I wait patiently but expectantly for the results of the discussions with the other congregation's Elders, the Circuit Overseer and the country's main branch. John takes the lead:

"It's been a tumultuous four weeks. We are really struggling with the attitudes of the Elders in your old congregation and the Circuit Overseer has had to step in to settle things down. We shouldn't really tell you that, but we wanted you to know how seriously we are taking this matter and demonstrate why things are taking so long."

I can feel myself sinking into my chair. This is all my fault. I'm ripping the Kingdom Hall apart. I can feel a voice in my head tell them to just forget it all and run like hell out of the Hall, but instead I sit here arguing again with myself internally.

"Now this is where we have been totally surprised by the reaction elsewhere," John continues. "Firstly, the Circuit Overseer tells us that under no circumstance are we to contact the Police."

My mum and dad give out an audible gasp and John has to put both his palms up in a gentle halting motion. "I know, I know we were really shocked as well. So, I telephoned the branch office and insisted that we have an opinion from them after giving them the details of your trauma. To our shock and surprise they said they had consulted their legal department and they whole heartedly agree that the Police should not be involved."

I cannot believe details of my discussions with the Elders in the congregation have gone out so far and to so many people. The Elders from the other congregation have told Alan, Bob and John. These have told the Circuit Overseer and now brothers at the branch office. I'm starting to feel like an emotional pinball. I want to stop the bus and get off, but the vehicle has a motion all its own where no one person seems to have control anymore.

I can see the embarrassment in John's eyes and the shame as he puts his head down and starts to read a letter in his hands and carries on relaying the branches findings. "The branch says that opening up accusations against a prominent brother in the congregation who has been found to be innocent by his judicial committee is bringing reproach against the accused, reproach against the congregation, reproach against the community of Jehovah's Witnesses and worse of all reproach against Jehovah. The accused did not have two witnesses to the alleged sin and therefore according to Bible law and rule he is not guilty. The matter should be closed immediately and the Elders who have brought these second accusations should be guided against pursuing such matters further in order to avoid actions being taken against them."

John's hands, with the letter gripped in his fingers, slams down onto his knees and his head looks up to the ceiling. I can almost see a tear welling in his eyes. I already felt ready to go home and now I'm certain that I have had enough of this. I look at my mum who has disappointment and sympathy in her eyes looking back at me.

This feels like the end of the runaway train. Part of me is relieved. I have tried at least to move forward for the sake of any other potential victims, but I cannot help but feel that I need to get on with another life. I have been through my worst hell already, lived it twice in fact. Facing being disfellowshipped and being treated like a disease is something I can survive with my parents supporting me and, although it's a different kind of suffering, it just isn't on the scale of what lies behind me.

The three Elders in the room look around at each other. There is silence in the room, and yet a visual discussion being held between the three of them. Something is hanging in the air. I can feel that these three have already been talking between themselves as they have a common look between them as they exchange glances with each other. The quiet seems to last forever. There are always pauses, there are silences, but this was a hush on the end of a precipice. I look around. I cannot stand the silence any longer and plan in my head to get up and ask to leave. As I let go of my mother's hand, Alan sees my move and, in an attempt to stop me, breaks the silence. "We must do it John. It's the right thing to do. If we are right God will look over us."

John nods and looks over at Bob who agrees with Alan.

John turns back to me.

"If it's ok with you, we all think that this matter is too serious not to go to the Police. Internal politics is getting in the way and if there are other victims, then they need our protection and they need to get professional help. We mean well, but when it comes to this, we are far from the experts that are needed. You have been so brave to go through, not only your awful experience, but to endure what else you have been put through by the Elders who are supposed to protect you and look after you. This cannot happen again, or even worse if it is still happening now, it must stop. We cannot ask anything more of you. You have done more than one lifetime's worth of good deeds. But if you will allow us, we want to get this stopped and report this matter to the Police. Will you allow us to do that?"

John delivered his question so softly, so caringly that it gave me a small amount of energy and a lift. Perhaps there is some kindness and love left here after all. I really did understand the subtext as well. They were not just reporting a crime to the Police, they were going to go rogue. I was a lowly, very young sister in the congregation. I was of no real importance and, as a woman, would never be significant in this male dominated world or in the political structure of the congregation. But an Elder is top of the food chain, a leader, someone you look up to. The sin would be perceived as so much greater to be disfellowshipped from their higher status, the shame so much more. The risk was as equally great as the threatened fall could be.

I shrugged it off. This must happen all the time. What kind of society would we have if nobody could ever question anything, especially when so clearly wrong? Surely Jehovah will see what is wrong and put the solutions in place.

I'm really moved as well that they have asked for my permission. At no point has anyone asked if I want to do anything through this whole nightmare, except my mum. I am so tired of it all. I want to just stop, go home and leave the world outside including my friends, outside family and everyone that doesn't talk to me now I'm disfellowshipped. My friends and family know me. They know that I am dedicated to Jehovah. Yet they just don't question at all – they just go along with one wrongdoing on top of another. I know they think they are doing it for me, to bring me back into the congregation clean and repentant. I've seen another side of the Society I belong to and I'm confused. I know there is a lot here that just isn't right. There is a lot that's so very wrong and immoral.

It's during that thought process, that, despite my wish to just stop this fight and supress my rebellion and rest, I start to think of the possibility of what Kris might be doing to other children in the congregation, perhaps even to some of my friends. My friends might not talk to me, but I do not want another person to experience this nightmare if it's within my small sphere of influence to stop it. I can feel the wind changing, I can feel my mind winning the internal battle and an inner energy rising up through me. I look straight at John.

"My body and mind say no, but my heart fights and says yes. I want to stop this and if reporting him will get him stopped then let's go to the Police."

Right on cue, as though God himself were angry, the storm outside breaks, a huge clap of thunder shakes the Kingdom Hall and the rain starts to pour loudly onto the building.

7 - AFRESH

That was four years ago.

I'm sitting on a beach. I have sand running in-between my fingers, the grains slowly pouring from the palm of my hand gently across each finger and onto the ground beside me. The sky above me is a deep, deep blue without a cloud to be seen. The warmth of the sun wraps me up and comforts me as I lie relaxed and relieved.

For a second, I wonder where I am, if I am really here. My brain goes into a spin and panic, suddenly aware that this is the same as the safe space in my imagination and hope that it hasn't been called upon again.

A calm washes over me, as I recall the airplane trip here and my partner lying next to me. This is nearly a perfect peace.

The journey has been a long and horrific one. That night when the storm broke was the last time that I went into a Kingdom Hall outside meetings. My journey split away from those three kind Elders, Alan, Bob and John. The Police investigated Kris and then arrested him not long after. Another two abused children were discovered, and Kris was charged with five counts of rape and child sex abuse.

Thankfully the other two victims never had to go through the shame of being interrogated by the Elders. They and I had lots of professional therapy.

It was during the court case that I learned of the word grooming. The Kingdom Hall had become the perfect place for ensnaring and threatening children with abuse and punishing them for even thinking about telling someone. It's like everyone in the congregation is part of a close and extended family. Those not related are still referred to as "aunts" and "uncles" by anyone a generation younger, even adults when talking to their peers. That close-knit community, as well as positions of trust, create the perfect breeding ground for the predator.

The families completely trust the "aunts" and "uncles" in the congregation, even with their own children. Ministerial Servants and Elders are not only trusted like family members but are also wholly appointed by God and so, in the minds of Jehovah's Witnesses families, can do no wrong because Jehovah has not only appointed them but would not allow his leaders to offend.

Kris then used that power and position to his advantage. He also made sure he picked out particular children. Ones that he could threaten with God's vengeance or fear of divine punishment or punishment from the Elders – those that would be fearful of him, the Elders and of God. He would remind them how sinful they are and how their punishment would be severe. How nobody would believe their word against his because of the trust he had in the congregation. He then used that power constantly, by words and even just by a look, to totally control those he abused to stay quiet and ashamed.

Kris was found guilty and got 30 years in prison.

The whole experience of working with the Police, of going through court and having to relive that same experience for a third time nearly killed me. Each low, each hit of depression never sunk to the nightmare of that first time because, at each point since, I have found less isolation. To have my parents with me and on my side saved my life. To know that I saved those other two children from having to suffer that awful experience, gave me some small solace that I had done the right thing. To know there are children that won't be Kris's victims has helped me see a bigger world.

Many other people's lives changed.

Sometimes I wonder if things could have been done any other way. That night was a catalyst for some massive changes that have impacted on so many other lives. After going to the Police and thus defying the orders of the Society of Jehovah's Witnesses, the three Elders, Alan, Bob and John all had their own Judicial Committees. They had to go through the same interrogation I had gone through, just to do right by me. I love all three of them.

They were all disfellowshipped and publicly disgraced. When the congregation was told of their sentence, many of their families and the brothers and sisters in the congregation knew why they had been disciplined and refused to shun their peers and loving colleagues. That induced another round of discipline which resulted in even more rebellion. Over half the congregation refused to accept the discipline of three men they all knew had acted with kindness, compassion and with good in their hearts.

The congregation was disbanded by the Circuit Overseer and the branch of Jehovah's Witnesses in the capital.

By the time all that fell apart, my family and I had stopped going to the Kingdom Hall. The national branch headquarters sent lawyers to defend Kris in court and lied many times in front of us all to protect an evil man. The trial, stripped anything that was left of our faith and left our souls in tatters. A huge portion of the disbanded congregation stopped being Jehovah's Witnesses as well and we all now meet up regularly as friends. It feels so good to know many good people are around us and that, if we look beyond our isolation, we have many brothers and sisters with a common experience. Good people.

I am by no means mended. I bleed and break many times. But I am no longer alone.

EPILOGUE

In 2012 the former Australian Prime Minister, the Hon. Julia Gillard, MP, announced the setting up of an Australian Royal Commission into Institutional Responses to Child Sexual Abuse. This Commission began work in 2013 and had a total budget of over $373 million. A part of the investigation covered the organisation of Jehovah's Witnesses in Australia.

The Commission subpoenaed the data from the headquarters of the Australian Jehovah's Witnesses organisation of reports of child abuse within its organisation. There were found to be 1006 cases. Of those 1006 case files. Of those 1006, not a single one had been reported to police.

The Australian Royal Commission concluded that the Jehovah's Witnesses organisation "does not respond adequately to child sexual abuse" and "fails to protect children".

Chief Justice McClellan, Chairperson of the Australian Royal Commission stated: "I don't know of any other organisation that has the flaws that we have identified in the Jehovah's Witnesses."

The Australian Royal Commission set up a National Redress Scheme on 1st July 2018 to help people who have experienced institutional child sexual abuse gain access to counselling, a direct personal response, and a redress payment.

Out of all the institutions that were named by the Australian Royal Commission, only 4 did not join the National Redress Scheme by the then deadline of 1st July 2020. One of those institutions are the Jehovah's Witnesses organisation. They have publicly refused to join the scheme.

In June 2020 the Jehovah's Witnesses organisation in Australia was accused of moving cash offshore to avoid paying abuse victims compensation.

Tens of millions of dollars are estimated to being paid out each year by the Jehovah's Witnesses organisation worldwide for legal settlements for abuse victims.

In July 2019 the District Court of Zurich, Switzerland, found that the religious practice of Jehovah's Witnesses violates the basic rights of their members, and:

- The practice of shunning exists and is at least to some extent a violation of human rights. Shunning can be understood as prescribed bullying and violates the integrity and implicit freedom of belief and conscience of the persons concerned.
- Children and young people too are affected by shunning. Children experience severe fear due to this religious practice.
- It still occurs repeatedly that Jehovah's Witnesses die as a result of the ban on blood transfusions.
- The "Two-Witness rule" exists along with other guidelines of the organisation which facilitate sexual abuse, especially of children

A call has been made on Swiss politicians to take action to review legislation and decide what political measures to take. Germany and Austrian governments have also been called on to explain why they, as States, approve religious guidelines that:

- Silence children and women affected by (sexual) violence,
- Call on parents to shun their underage children and
- Abandon people whose lives are in danger

We are living in a time of unsung heroes. There are survivors of abuse that are fighting the system and exposing the wrong done to them and others around them. There are support networks growing around the world run by kind people dedicated to saving the lives of those harmed and rejected by dangerous cults. There are people bravely standing up to the bullies, pointing straight at them, at great personal cost, and highlighting their hypocrisy, lies and greed in public forums worldwide. There are people supporting and representing cult abuse survivors in the courts all over the earth.

They are all superheroes and have earned our attention and praise.

ABOUT THE AUTHOR

Jonny Halfhead grew up as a third generation Jehovah's Witness and remained one for twenty years, becoming thoroughly immersed in its doctrines and practices. Although never baptised, he was raised under a very strict regime that always made him different and stand out from everyone else around him, even others in the same faith.

When circumstances ejected him from that controlling and all-encompassing lifestyle, he was in a unique position to follow his love of music and expand his imagination as an all-round artist. Jonny Halfhead started a Gothic music fanzine in the early nineties, joined a band called 13 Candles and then formed his own band called Personality Crisis in 1994.

In 2012 Jonny Halfhead started an online blog about his hobby of collecting the music of the famous independent music label 4AD with the aim on exhibiting his collection on the labels 50th anniversary in 2030. After a few years the blog entries started to dwindle as it became more difficult to collect and stick to the high expectations and costs placed he placed upon his own collection promise.

In 2018 Jonny Halfhead released his first short story "Nine Pills" through Amazon, which had many elements based on his youth as being one of Jehovah's Witnesses and the struggles involved with being associated with a cult. A few months later he released another short story "The 1975 Apocalypse" which once again drew on his experiences as a Jehovah's Witness from his youth.

Now he has written a third fictional short story "The Offence of Grace" which highlights the problem of institutional child sex abuse in his former religion.

For support with leaving the Jehovah's Witnesses organization or any of the issues raised in this book please visit
https://xjwfriends.com/

Edited by Setters Proofreading and Editing Services

www.jonnyhalfhead.com

Printed in Poland
by Amazon Fulfillment
Poland Sp. z o.o., Wrocław

61788365R00061